More Stories That Won't Make Your Parents Hurl

For Laura,
It's good
for kids
to be
scared!

2007

Edited by Selina Rosen

ISBN 1-893687-42-2

Yard Dog Press
710 W. Redbud Lane
Alma, AR 72921-7247

http://www.yarddogpress.com

Edited by Selina Rosen
Copy Editor Leonard Bishop
Technical Editor Lynn Stranathan
Cover and interior art by Marziah Karch

Printed in the United States of America
0 9 8 7 6 5 4 3 2 1

Table of Contents

Introduction

This book is unashamedly children's horror in the age-old tradition of scaring children into good behavior.

Many modern psychiatrists I'm sure would say this is wrong. However, I always say, "If it ain't broke, don't fix it!" and parents have always used scare tactics when dealing with their kids.

Besides, I think it's sort of hypocritical for society as a whole to bash the old Grimm brothers' fairytales as being too graphic and too frightening for kids, and then condone – even fully support – the anti-drug and tobacco ads we see on TV every day. You've got ads in which human bodies are thrown around. If that's not horror, I don't know what is.

Plain and simple, there are more things that damage children and society than drugs and cigarettes.

I chose the stories in this collection not only because they were well written, and highly entertaining, but because they encompassed a full spectrum of "dos" and "don'ts" that every 21st century child needs to learn. It covers everything from firearm safety and petty thievery to dental hygiene and animal cruelty.

Some of the children in these stories are heroes; some are villains. But most are just plain kids who make some bad decisions and have to pay for their actions. It's all about action and consequence in this book. No stories where someone does something wrong, but Mom and Dad hug them and tell them they love them anyway, and the problem just goes away.

That just isn't the way the real world works, and why do we insist on teaching our children that it is? Eventually they have to go into the real world, and our job as parents is to prepare them for that time. I contend that you don't do that by reading them some sappy little politically correct book that teaches them that no matter how badly you mess up, everything will somehow magically pop right back into place.

Some of these writers are old hands in this craft, some are brand new, but all of them know how to tell a good story. Some of the stories are geared to younger children, and some, obviously, to older children. I suggest you read them yourself first to make sure it won't give your child nightmares. For instance, Rob Gates' "The Empty Plate," or Tracy Morris' "Paratroop Bear" could be read to any five year old. However, Greg Burnham's "Tray Man," or Garrett Peck's "Puppy Love" would only be appropriate for the most secure child under ten.

These stories have been purposely crafted to appeal to the adult reading them as much as the child they are being read to. In fact, I'd go so far as to say that if your child went to sleep while you were reading one of these stories, you'd have to go ahead and finish it yourself.

A Knight of Swords

by

William D. Gagliani

For Alistair MacLean
And in memory of my grandparents

When I heard the soft knock against the loose paneling in the basement, I had just finished checking to make sure my parents' bedroom door was closed. They were talking in there, and it didn't sound so good. It was probably about me. And what they were gonna do with me. Again. But at least they were busy right now, and that's all I cared about. Until that knocking started up again, and it almost made me jump out of my skin. Even mice don't knock in that *tum-tum-tadum-tum-tumtum* pattern, you know?

I was creeping around silently in the basement wearing only an old pair of pajamas and my stupid fuzzy rabbit slippers. I had been working on my hideout for a week. It was a little igloo made of boxes and crates pushed up against the paneling along the back wall, and it was a great place to hide out when my folks wanted to find me. Punishments and chores. Chores and punishments. Ho hum.

God, I was tired of that!

Then the knocking started again –

tum-tum-tadum-tum-tumtum

– and the scenes of some zombie movie flashed through my brain. I was sitting there in the dark, and maybe half-decayed arms were gonna come through that wall, bloody claws grabbing for my throat, dragging me close enough for some zombie to chomp on my face!

If I jumped on out of there, I'd make so much noise that my folks would have me and my hideout all figured.

But if I stayed ...

tum-tum-tadum-tum-TumTum!

I didn't have time to turn on the light.

No zombie was gonna get me! I scooped a long wooden rod from the corner of my igloo where I'd left it and gripped it in both hands. Listening.

All I could hear was the new ticking furnace, which was on the other side of my hiding place. Maybe the whole thing was my imagination, or the furnace, or maybe —

TUM-TUM-TADUM-TUM-TUMTUM!!

That was it! I stabbed out with the wooden rod, expecting to maybe feel the dead arms of some slouching, slobbering creature. But instead I gave the paneling a loud *THWACK!* and something slid open and before I knew it I was falling forward into a hole that wasn't there a second before. I dropped the piece of wood and there was a loud metallic *clang.*

"What the-"

My knees hurt where I'd skinned them on the stone steps. *Stone steps? What stone steps?*

The staircase was dim, but not totally dark. It was lit by the faraway glow of a lantern or candle, about twenty steps down. Clumps of mud lay on the top step, right where I'd gone sprawling.

How could there be a stone staircase under my basement?

"Uh, I'm very sorry, Sire."

"Ah!" I jumped back and almost went flying into the muddy sludge. The voice came out of the dark right behind me, where I'd fallen through the panel that had opened up. But now I couldn't see the hole, and there was somebody standing there, in the dark.

I almost swallowed my tongue trying to speak. "What – who are you? What is this place?"

You might think that took some guts, but the voice *did* apologize after all. Maybe I could get close enough to kick him where it would hurt the most!

"I am Grawynn, Sire, and I'm to be your squire. Let me help you to your feet."

A hand shot out of the dark. I reached down and grabbed my only weapon, the wooden rod I had dropped. But it was gone. In its place there was this huge broadsword with a shimmering blue-green jewel set into the hilt. The edges looked pretty sharp, so I figured this was even better than the rod. It was heavy, too, but I heaved it and waved it into the weirdo's face. Then he stepped out of the dark, and he didn't seem so weird after all. Just a scrawny guy in some kind of Sherwood Forest outfit with bits of leather and metal sticking out here and there. He had a sword, too, a smaller one at his side. He got on his knees, right in the mud.

"Sire," he said, "please forgive the intrusion into your world, but the Council needs you and I have been sent by Caliburn himself to fetch you. It is a dire matter, Sire, and only you can help us!" Then he bowed low.

I liked that. I liked that *a lot*.

"Tell me more," I said. The sword was starting to feel good in my hands. For a second I wished my parents could see me, but they were probably too busy planning a punishment for my latest stunt.

Still on his knees, he gushed, "Sire, you hold the hand and a half sword forged for you by Caliburn himself. You are to be our greatest hero. And —" he stopped to catch his breath.

"Yeah? Spill it!"

"It's the Jewelled Sword, Sire," he blurted out. "The Dark Lord's stolen it from the Tower!"

I almost helped him to his feet, but then I decided I should keep talking down to him. After all, I *was* taller than him. And he was calling *me* Sire, not the other way around.

I lowered the sword. It was getting heavy. "Who's this Dark Lord, anyway?"

"A creature of the night, I'm afraid. That's why I came to you!"

I smiled. This was just too cool. If this guy wasn't a wacko, I was about to get some cool hero gig. And all because of that loose panel in the basement of our new house.

After my Dad got fired from his job, he went through a retraining program and my Mom went back to work, too. Things got difficult, I guess. I don't much like to talk about it, cause then they started getting on my case a lot. Like, all the time. It got so I couldn't do anything right. Then we moved to the midwest, where they both could work and save more. Our new house was actually old, a "damn fixer-upper" Dad called it, with four huge bedrooms and a library and a den and a full dining room, and an old-fashioned pantry. And a dingy basement that still had a neat old billiard table and bar all built-in by a previous owner who had tried to liven the place up. Failed though, cause it was still dingy. And then my dad sold the billiard table and put in the new furnace. "You have to learn to do without some things in life," he had said on the day they carted off the table. Yeah, sure.

"What if I don't feel like helping you?"

His face got all scrunched up in the dim light and I almost laughed. It was like he couldn't think of anything to say. "But, you have to help us, Sire! It's part of the Prophecy."

There's that "have to" again. Ugh.

I hate to "have to" do anything.

"Prophecy?"

"Yes, Sire. It says that once a generation we will need a champion, a hero, and through that doorway there lives someone who is destined to be that hero. You are the one, and I was sent to summon you, but so far I have had no luck."

The folks who lived in the house before us left very quickly. Maybe they wanted no part of this destiny deal. Tough crap for *them*. This seemed like the kind of place I could get some respect.

"What's your name again?" I asked.

"Grawynn, Sire."

"Get up, Grawynn." As he started to rise, I said. "No, wait. Stay down." And he did!

Cool! My every word was like a command to this guy. Heh, and I could give a *lot* of commands!

Some people might not like all this power. But I did. I could never be cool at school, and my folks were too busy with their own problems to really notice me unless they had some work for me to do, or I was in trouble, but here – here I was somebody special!

"Up, up!" He almost fell over himself trying to get up.

"So now what?" I asked.

He pointed down the staircase. There were trees down there! And I thought I heard horses stamping and huffing. This was getting better and better. "Lead the way," I said, and as I followed, I felt my fuzzy slippers harden into tough leather boots and my pajamas somehow turned into lightweight armor trimmed with strips of silver-studded leather. I must have made some sound, because Grawynn stopped and smiled.

"Yes, the translation spell is working on you. It's what gave you the sword you now call your own."

"What's so important about this, uh, Jewelled Sword?" I asked Grawynn as he led us down the stairs. Sure enough, the woods stretched out as far as I could see. And there were two huge horses standing a few feet away, one so white it hurt to look at him, and one dark brown chestnut.

Grawynn handed me a large, rough lump of sugar. "The white one is yours, Sire. Make his acquaintance."

I'd been on a horse before, and this one seemed to know it. He nuzzled my hand, and I gave the big stallion the sugar cube. "What's his name?"

"He is yours to name, Sire."

What else could I name him? "Silver," I said, as I fed

him another lump Grawynn handed me and rubbed his broad head. His eyes were huge and seemed to look right into me. Man, that made me nervous! But then I felt as if we'd always known each other, and I knew that as long as I gave him sugar and didn't mistreat him, he'd be loyal only to me. I wondered *how* I knew that, but it was as if the thought got injected into my head!

"What about that sword you were talking about?"

"The Jewelled Sword contains all the magic of the Realm, Sire."

"Well, that's pretty stupid, isn't it?" I blurted out.

Grawynn looked down. "Perhaps, but it just is ... no one here has had a choice in making it so."

"Whatever. Go on, don't stop talking!"

"Sorry, Sire. All our kings and barons respect its power and its very presence has kept us free from true war for centuries. But now the Dark Lord has returned and, with the sword in his hand, war will follow. Minor squabbles have already broken out among barons of the Lowlands."

"Why can't we punish them?" I thought about my parents, and how they never listen to my side of anything – they just hand down punishments. Maybe these baron-guys could be handled the same way.

"They are barons, Sire, not children! And it's not just barons. Kings have been shouting at each other more often than usual. If the Dark Lord learns to use the sword's magic, chaos will erupt."

"Humph," I said. Maybe I'd just have to *order* that the barons be punished.

"We must ride, Sire." He climbed onto his horse and waited for me. I noticed that neither horse was tied up.

There was an empty scabbard hanging from Silver's saddle, so I sheathed my sword in it then swung myself up. The horse nodded as if he agreed. "Where are we heading?"

Grawynn stroked his horse's mane and whispered in its ear. I gathered her name was Garnet. Then he turned to me. "Caliburn himself has asked to meet and instruct you."

"Didn't you say this Caliburn dude made *my* sword?" I said as we set off at a gallop.

"And the Jewelled Sword, as well. He is our most powerful and revered wizard. Only he knows how the magic works, but he is too old to fight the Dark Lord. That is why we need a champion."

This beats sleep any day, I thought as Grawynn took us

through the dark woods for several hours. *Or doing chores my dad's too lazy to do himself.* We rode through a half dozen deserted villages – where were all the grinning happy people that should have been hanging around? It was like the cute little thatched-roof cottages had all turned into run-down shacks. Even the trees seemed to hunker down with depression, and their leaves were either washed-out or downright brown. The evergreens looked droopy. Everything was ugly, but you got the feeling it wasn't supposed to be. There was something in the air, and it reminded me of the atmosphere at home when my folks were fighting, or having one of their *little talks* with me. I didn't like it one bit.

We didn't talk as we rode. Then we climbed a hill along a narrow, rocky path, and suddenly we were there.

Caliburn's castle rose out of the ground all of a sudden, but it was mostly in ruins. Only one of four towers still stood, and half of that seemed ready to crumble at any time. If that was Caliburn himself, waiting for us at the castle gates, he seemed ancient and infinitely weary. He was all stooped over and needed a knotted cane to hold himself up. You'd think a great wizard could keep himself young.

"It is good you have come, Young Sire," he said in a voice that was still strong. "It is my pleasure to meet you, our newest champion from the other world. Many times have we needed someone like you in our past, and we thank you!"

"Whatever. What's with this sword that's missing, and this dark guy who took it?"

The old man raised an eyebrow. He reminded me of my dad, just before he'd start to get all mad about something. "Every moment we waste the Dark Lord comes closer to understanding the magic of the Jewelled Sword, symbol of our peace for many decades."

"Yeah, so my squire says. So what do you want from me?" I slid off Silver's back before Grawynn could move. He looked disappointed, but what do I care if it's his job to fuss over me? I don't need help – I'm the hero guy around here.

"Only you can stop the Dark Lord," said Caliburn, trying to be patient, "because he is one of yours. And he hopes to learn the sword's magic to help him enslave your world."

"One of mine?" I hate when old dudes talk in hobbit-like riddles. Just spit it out, man! I think I'll get a tattoo that says that.

"He has always been powerful in your world. Your idle hands are his workshop. He nudges your leaders to poor decisions and dark deeds. He offers you more than you are capable of taking, and he corrupts your good thoughts with evil ones."

I was beginning to catch his drift. "You mean like the devil?"

"That is but one name by which he is known."

"Cool!"

"I daresay not!"

"How can I stop him then? He's gotta be too powerful for me. I mean, Satan! The devil! Can't you help? You're like the big wizard around here, right? This is your fight too, isn't it?"

Caliburn leaned on his cane and sighed. "I did help, when I forged the Jewelled Sword and sealed within it the magic that would keep our worlds safely separate. And I helped when I forged your magic sword, Young Sire." He mumbled something else, but I ignored him.

"Magic, huh?" I looked at my hand and a half sword, sheathed on Silver's saddle. It seemed ordinary, you know, like a cool dragon-slaying sword in the movies. Who woulda figured there was magic in it beyond whatever turned it from a piece of wood into a sword. Just like this old guy to keep it a secret. Adults never tell kids anything.

"More magic than you can possibly imagine. In fact, without *your* sword, the Jewelled Sword cannot work its own magic. And the Dark Lord cannot remove it from here without your sword to unlock the protective spell."

"You mean –"

"Yes, he will seek you out and challenge you, and you must win, or he will have both swords and the magic will be his to unleash upon all the worlds – and there are infinitely more worlds than you know, boy."

Who said I wanted to challenge somebody called the Dark Lord, who was maybe even more than just a really bad guy? And if he really was the devil ...? I had some thinking to do, but I didn't much like the way things were going.

"But then why do you want me here?" I said. "If he couldn't get to my sword while it was back in my world, he would never have been able to bring the swords together ..."

"Silly boy," snarled Caliburn, "in *your* world, your puny sword is merely a piece of useless wood. But here, here it is the other half of Caliburn's twisted joke upon me!"

And then Caliburn's face melted away like wax and rotting skin and it wasn't the old wizard Caliburn at all, but a huge horned creature twenty feet tall with red, burning eyes and steam rising from his scaly skin. A reptilian tail swung back and forth behind him, twitching like a snake. At the tip of the tail was a snake's head, complete with hissing tongue and curved fangs, some kind of slimy drool trailing onto the ground and burning wherever it touched. The cane had turned into a mean blade that had to be a foot wide and sparkled with rows of jewels.

The horses reared and backed off, and Grawynn hit the dirt next to me, trying to dig himself a hole to crawl into. Fat lotta good *he* was!

My knees wobbled. My light armor seemed heavy and useless now. I had no magic, and I knew the creature before me knew it.

I would have given anything to be able to open my eyes and find that this had all been a nightmare, and that the sun was peeking cheerfully through the shades in my room. My own ordinary ridiculous little room. Even when grounded and held prisoner, it was heaven compared to this disgusting thing in front of me.

The Dark Lord snarled down at me, one taloned claw slowly reaching out as I froze in my footsteps.

"Where is the real Caliburn?" I shouted at the creature from Hell itself. "What have you done with him?"

The Dark Lord laughed, and it was so chilling a sound that Grawynn groaned and fainted, and Garnet bolted. Silver reared, but stood by me, his hoofs pounding the muddy turf.

Silver knew about my destiny, and the sword!
I didn't know why, but I could feel it.

"The old magician is locked up in the tower, foolish one! I would have used him to force your hand, had you not been so easy to deceive."

His laugh boomed out over the land, and I felt the trees in the woods shivering with fear. All I could do was hope this great wizard Caliburn was okay, and that the Dark Lord had told me some truth during his arrogant little charade. But if it was all a crock, then we were all in some deep dung.

Grawynn struggled to his knees. "I'm sorry, Sire, but I..."

I was about to help him up, until I remembered what our relationship is supposed to be. He was *my* squire. "Get my sword, Grawynn," I said with as much calm as I could manage – which wasn't much, but it must have been enough because he got a hold of himself.

"Yes, Sire!" His eyes gleamed. Maybe I looked more like a champion all of a sudden.

Silver edged closer and more or less pushed the sword's

leather-wrapped grip into Grawynn's hand.   Grawynn
unsheathed the sword and exclaimed in awe as the long blade
immediately started to glow. He handed it to me and you should
have seen it glow then! It was as if my touch had somehow
activated the magic the *real* Caliburn had forged into the blade.

I held up the sword and stared straight at the towering
horror of the Dark Lord.

I gulped. His eyes were like laser cannons, but this wasn't
any video game I had ever played. Even in Doom, you don't
really get killed. This hero stuff wasn't all it was cracked up to
be.

*"Prepare to match blades with me, evil one, as foretold by the
Old Ones in their infinite wisdom!"*

Yup, those words poured out of my mouth like water,
but I had no idea where they came from. It was almost like reading
someone else's speech – it still makes sense, but the words sound
strange in your own ears.

"Blast you, boy!" the Dark Lord boomed and fireballs
spit from his mouth. "You have learned the words of power!"

Grawynn whispered something behind me.

"Caliburn worked them into the sword's spell," I shouted,
and charged. Get this, *I* charged at *him*. I still can't believe I did
that. Usually I avoid bullies, unless they're smaller than me.

We locked blades in a shower of unearthly sparks. The
impact rattled my teeth and drove me backward, and I would
have ended up on my back, except I smacked right into Silver,
who whinnied in my ear and nudged my head. I looked up. The
Dark Lord loomed over me, his huge sword held high over his
head.

I felt something wrap around my ankles. The demon's
serpent tail was slithering up my
shin, red lidless eyes staring into
mine, mouth open and huge fangs
dripping acid saliva that ate
through my armor, scorching my
skin.

I screamed like a girl in a
crappy horror movie, I know I did.

And before I knew what I
was doing, I sliced downward and
cut right through the tail. I saw
the snake head go flying in a gross
cloud of squirting greenish blood,
and then the Dark Lord shrieked

in pain and I had to parry upward with my blade because he was smashing his sword down on me like an axe over and over. I felt the sparks burn into my skin and I have to tell you, right then I didn't much like the idea of being anyone's champion any more.

The Dark Lord's fake Caliburn features had all melted like wax – now he was just an ugly, disgusting demon four times as big as I was. *And his sword was hammering me into the ground.*

Behind me, Silver whinnied again. And then he was up on his hind legs, his front hoofs slicing into the demon's face until the Dark Lord screamed with pain and rage. I used this diversion to get out from under the demon's sword blows, though I could barely roll out of the way. There was a solid *clang* as his sword glanced off one of my angled shoulder plates and I rolled the other way and – for one strange, long second – *I looked right into Silver's eyes and saw in them the answer, the knowledge I needed.*

I still don't know how I realized it, but I did.

Silver stepped back, letting me take over.

I hoped I was right — that I *had* seen the answer there. Because otherwise I was toast.

The demon's breath was hot and disgusting on my face, and I barely had time to roll away again before the Jewelled Sword came down and sank into the mud right next to my head. Before he could pull it free, I was up and behind him. He turned with a growl, and that was when I touched his blade with mine and said the words that came to me in a flash of inspiration:

Bind these strong blades as one!

Suddenly the two swords began to tremble and vibrate like giant magnets. I held on to mine with both hands, while the Jewelled Sword slid slowly out of the Dark Lord's grip, attaching itself to the metal of my blade. Weird blue light played around my arms and the swords, and the Dark Lord's expression changed from ferocious to fearful.

They just popped into my head, so I spoke more words from a memory I didn't have:

Begone then, spawn of darkness;
Take your evil from our land
In the name of Justice and Right.
I bind thee within these blades;
Banished to metal, entrapped by this spell
Reversible only by a true knight of swords!

Thunder crashed overhead and a violent wind rushed through with a loud roaring, almost snapping off the trees around us. The ground shook for a long moment, then seemed to settle. I saw the Dark Lord's mouth open in a long and silent scream of rage and fear, and then he was gone. Just like that. The sudden silence slashed into my eardrums and my ears popped, like on a landing jet.

The fused swords burned in my hand and I yelped and dropped them. When I bent down to pick them up, I noticed that now they seemed more like one sword, a giant Jewelled Sword with a design engraved on it. I looked more closely at the design.

It was an etching of the Dark Lord – but his eyes moved and stared right at me!

The Dark Lord was imprisoned in the swords, and I had put him there by saying words I didn't even know I knew.

"That is correct."

I whirled and saw only Grawynn and Silver, but then the great white horse seemed to go blurry and I realized that his lips were moving. But they didn't look like horse lips any more. And where Silver had stood, now there was a bearded man wearing a simple cloth cape.

"*Caliburn?*" I gasped.

The old sword-maker nodded. "Sometimes we know not who sets rules, nevertheless we follow them. That is destiny, young one, and yours was to defeat this great enemy. You knew how to do it, but you needed nudging. And he could not bind *all* my magic!"

Grawynn looked as though he would have fainted, but instead all he did was grin like a fool.

The woods around us seemed to be coming to life – people stepped out of the dark undergrowth and surrounded us, laughing like I always thought people here would be doing. Then I was grinning, too. What the hell, they loved me! Caliburn smiled and spread his arms.

"Take the newly-forged Jewelled Sword, young knight, and keep it safe in your care." Everyone cheered. I blushed all the way down to my toes. No one ever cheered for me at home. No one even noticed me, unless police cars were involved. This felt pretty good.

We partied for days, and tremendous fun was had by all.

Then the cheering faded, and I left them all behind. It was time to go home – I needed a shower and my mom's cooking. I needed to hear some loud Kid Rock. I needed to check my e-mail. I climbed the mossy stairs and reached the portal. It was strange, but the local folks and Grawynn had all stopped cheering and making noise. I turned and almost bumped into Caliburn, who must have come up silently behind me.

"What is it?"

"Nothing, young knight. You are one of us, now."

"Yeah, sure, see ya later. Call me when you need me again, okay?" I reached for the door, but my fingers brushed cobwebs and dusty old wood and stone. There was no handle, no knob, no way to get the door open. "Hey!" I tore fingernails on the planks and rough rock. "What's going on? I can't find the door! It was *here*, right here ..."

Caliburn's voice swept over me like doom itself. "There is no longer a door. The portal is closed. We've found the hero we needed this generation, and now you must remain here with us."

"What? Forever?"

"Forever."

"No way!" I shouted, and put my shoulder to the door that used to be there, right there. My fingers were bloody when I finally stopped trying to find the edge of the entrance back to where I came from. I could feel tears forming in my eyes, then running down my cheeks. I never thought I'd want to go home as badly as I did that second. When I'd been there, all I wanted was to be gone, and to get some respect. Now I had respect, all right, but I didn't want the job that went with it.

"But I belong there," I said weakly. "My parents –"

"You didn't much care for your parents, according to our information. And besides, we've taken care of that part," Caliburn said mysteriously. "They won't miss you. In fact, they'll wonder at how obedient their son Lance has become. And how studious."

"But I haven't! I'm just as lousy a kid as I ever was! I hate your guts!" I stood up and made a pair of blood-ugly fists. Caliburn snarled and made a single quick motion, and I was sitting down on the steps.

"You'll be too busy to be a lousy kid," he said. "You have daily sword practice, riding lessons, language lessons, courtesy lessons, and lessons on learning your lessons."

"But-but-"

Caliburn cocked his head. "Then you'll be busy fighting some of this gentle land's worst enemies. The Four Horsemen approach even now, having been joined by a Fifth, the first cousin of Pestilence. My spies have informed me that an evil scientist plans to create a race of super vampires and conquer us. And there have been rumblings from the deep caverns on the other side of the mountains – it seems the angry giant we entombed there a thousand years ago is awakening. You are our hero now, therefore all of these have become a part of your duties. You-"

I didn't hear anything else he had to say. I was too busy screaming and screaming, hopeless, frightened, and very alone.

-end-

On "A Knight of Swords" & William D. Gagliani

"A Knight of Swords" grew partly out of my fascination with Arthurian legend. I did part of my Master's work in medieval literature, and I always intended to write Arthurian stories of my own. But I've spent most of my time in the horror field, so I put it off. Now here's my chance to introduce my young knight and his Arthurian adventures, which owe a little something to contemporary fantasy, too, because the magic takes place in a world parallel to ours. Like so many kids today, my reluctant hero avoids responsibility and hard work, but thinks he deserves more respect from his parents. He doesn't realize how good he has it until he doesn't have it. He's smart and sarcastic, but would probably grow up to be a slacker if he didn't end up a heroic knight, fighting for his life against weird creatures in a troubled magical realm. Stay tuned.

I was born in the States, but grew up in Italy in Genova, the hometown of Christopher Columbus. Since the age of four, all I've ever wanted to be was a writer — Jules Verne made sure of that. When I'm not writing or reading, reviewing books, or watching movies, I'm the Stacks Supervisor at Marquette University's Memorial Library in Milwaukee, where I live with the love of my life, Janis, and way too many books. I collect weird weapons and progressive rock recordings, and I'm a failed wanna-be prog-rock keyboard player with more toys than talent!

My e-book collection of stories, *Shadowplays*, is available from www.Ebooksonthe.net. I've had stories in anthologies such as *Robert Bloch's Psychos, Extremes 3: Terror On The High Seas, Extremes 4: Darkest Africa, Bubbas of the Apocalypse, The Midnighters Club, The Asylum 2: The Violent Ward,* and *More Monsters From Memphis.* My nonfiction has been published in *Cemetery Dance, BookPage,* The Chiaroscuro (website), *BookLovers, Science Fiction Chronicle, Horror Magazine,* and others.

(Look for William's new book, *Wolf's Trap,* coming from Yard Dog Press late in 2003.)

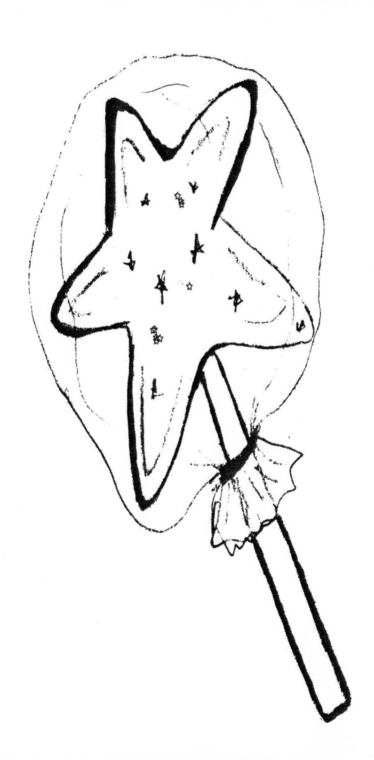

SUCKER

by
Philip Robinson

When you stood in the side-room of Old Rosa's house, just off the entrance-hall, the rest of the world disappeared. You didn't care about teachers, parents, bullies, chores...all you cared about were suckers. And if you cared about suckers, Old Rosa's house was the place to be.

The candy came in all different shapes, sizes, and colors. There were wicker baskets standing around the floor, overflowing with red'n'yellow spirals, glazed-honey suns and creamy-white moons, long slabs of jelly and twisting macaroon corkscrews. There were big Indian snake-charmer baskets brimming with fiery candy of endless flavors. Strawberry, raspberry, blueberry, blackberry, raisin, grape, vanilla, watermelon, peanut-butter, tutti-frutti, apple, orange, pear, banana, peach, grape, tomato, cookiedough, chocolate, cola, Dr. Pepper, rootbeer, Sprite, cream soda, Irish Cream.

Kids were running around, squealing with delight while Old Rosa pottered through the room...tidying displays which didn't need tidying and chatting to the children.

William selected a 'Watermelon Shark'. One of his favorites. Then a 'Prickly Pear' – a sour-pear ball with a spiky surface which left the tongue feeling itchy and burned, but once you sucked away the spines there was a big fizzy ball at the center which exploded in your mouth. The next one he selected was a 'Golden Nugget' – a rectangular block of sour lemon, and this one he deftly slipped into his coat pocket while Old Rosa was busy serving some kids at the small counter.

The suckers were a dollar each, and every Saturday morning William would come here, buy three, and steal two. Why not? He bought more than any other kid so he should be getting a special deal, shouldn't he? She wasn't really losing out that much. They probably only cost her twenty cents to make, so she was still making a tidy profit...and a couple of suckers disappearing into his pocket once a week...she wouldn't even notice.

He wandered a little more, picking up and sniffing various plastic wrappings, then selected a 'Black Widow' – a licorice spider the size of his hand with red sour-cherry eyes and white, milky fangs. He would pay for this one.

He moved in the general direction of the counter, a hand pressed against his pocket making sure the stolen sucker was safely tucked inside. Old Rosa was laughing at a little girl who couldn't even wait to get outside before opening the sucker she'd bought.

There was a large basket off to the side of the counter. Inside was a cluster of big, black stars...with blue streaks running through them like waves and each flecked with nuggets of gold and silver which glimmered and sparkled in the light. There were strings of colored candy trailing down like comet-tails, longer than the sticks the suckers were on. The sign above the basket said, "Stardust Special: $10".

Ten bucks. He picked one up and turned it around in his hand, and each movement caused the gold and silver to flash as though alive. Ten bucks. He sniffed at it but couldn't smell anything through the wrapping. He glanced at Old Rosa, who had her back to him while she made change, and in a flash the 'Stardust Special' was deep in his pocket.

He went to the counter and put his three suckers down, along with three dollars. "What are those like?" he asked, glancing at the basket of ten-dollar suckers. For the first time since the first time, he felt a little nervous.

Rosa sighed. "Oh....I cannot describe how they taste. But I would not ask for ten dollars if they weren't worth at least twenty!"

Sitting on a hill in the park, looking down on the lake, today there was no question which sucker he'd have first.

For a moment he just held it up in front of his face and watched the gold and silver shine...probably just lumps of coloured sugar, but with Old Rosa nothing was 'just pieces of sugar'. This was going to be something special.

When he tore the wrapper away, the smell of the sucker rushed into his nose and inflamed his brain. He could wait no longer. He stuck out his tongue and greedily licked the sucker. The taste exploded in his mouth. The texture was smooth and glassy, but the little flecks of silver and gold tickled and chafed his tongue and ignited sensations he hadn't even known his tastebuds could feel. He licked the sucker like a kitten lapping milk, fireworks exploding inside his mouth, electricity surging through his tongue, and when he finally allowed his teeth to crack that glassy exterior he found the inside soft and chewy, a warm texture which almost melted on his tongue. It was both sour and very sweet, and the juices which ran down his throat were like the cream of a sweet dessert. He bit and chewed and sucked and licked, making sure to get every little piece from the stick.

And then it was gone.

William almost cried. He ran his tongue along his teeth and gums, trying to suck out every last iota of taste. The Stardust Special was gone.

As he walked home, he thought about how he might go about getting another one.

His mom was busy in the kitchen so he didn't bug her. Asking for money when she was busy meant a definite 'No'. He decided to wait until after dinner to make his move.

Pizza. One ham and pineapple; one loaded with meat. In the living room, he took the armchair. There was some silly show starting on television but he wasn't paying it any attention. He wanted so much to ask Mom, but he couldn't just blurt it out in front of Helen, his younger sister. He took a big bite of his pizza. Later Mom would be in the kitchen by herself, washing dishes and then maybe –

William suddenly gagged, and spat out the lump of pizza he'd bitten off. A loud belch ripped from his throat. Mom and Helen were gaping at him. He quickly got up and ran to the kitchen, and put his plate down on the table. Just the steaming ham'n'pineapple pizza, yet the taste had been like...revolting, disgusting. It tasted...*burnt* somehow, except much worse than that.

Mom was peering out at him through the kitchen door. He took the second, untouched piece from the plate. It looked fine, smelled perfect....

He nibbled and found it was deli –

Awful!!!

His stomach lurched, as though forewarning him to not even try sending some of that hideous stuff down!

Quickly, he poured a glass of cola...anything to get the horrible taste away...and gulped it. But when the soft drink filled his mouth it tasted like cold, fizzy soup and he spewed out the mouthful, his stomach revolted and he threw up on the floor. Mom and Helen rushed into the kitchen while he crouched down on hands and knees.

In a flurry, Mom brought him into the living room and sat him on the sofa. He felt a little queasy; his head ached. Helen got him a drink of water which he greedily devoured, enjoying its tasteless quality.

"Some color's coming back into your face now," Mom said. "Go lie down for a while. Best thing for you."

He did as he was told, and upstairs he slumped onto his bed, staring at the ceiling.

Maybe he was just feeling guilty? But he'd been taking two freebies every Saturday for so long...why would he start suddenly feeling guilty now? He lay there long enough for his brain to half-convince him it had all been his imagination, and he began feeling hunger pangs in his stomach.

His jacket was hanging on the end of the bed and he reached into the pockets and took out the other four suckers from Old Rosa's. These were suckers he'd had a million times before, and he knew what they were supposed to taste like.

He opened the 'Black Widow', the paper crinkling as he tore it away, and held it in front of his face. He could smell the liquorice...it would be soft and chewy and delicious. The red eyes would erupt in explosions of sour-cherry fire, and the fangs would burst with milky sweetness.

Cautiously, he licked the spider's belly and his tongue immediately recoiled from the taste. He flung it across the room and tried to spit the taste out of his mouth. Just like the gag-inducing pizza and cola, it made his stomach clench like a fist inside him. Again that taste of something half-rotten and burnt, something gut-churning.

He lay back, a light sheen of perspiration on his face, breath coming urgently, gasping.

Sunday morning, he went downstairs.

In the kitchen, he got a glass of water and gulped it down. Perfect and pure. No taste.

He went to the fridge and poured himself a glass of milk. It looked cool and refreshing. He'd try it, and if it was okay he'd try it on a bowl of cereal. He lifted the glass to his lips, taking in that slight aroma of fresh milk, and then sipped it.

(retch!)

With a shaking hand he slammed the glass down on the counter and spit the small sip of rancid, sour milk into the sink. It had felt lumpy in his mouth, sharply bitter and not like milk at all.

"Hey," his mom said, coming into the kitchen. "Feeling better?"

"Thought I could drink a glass of milk, but I guess my stomach's not ready yet."

"Oh well, don't force it." She picked up the glass of milk. "No point in letting it go to waste." She downed it in one gulp.

William knew he couldn't sit around all day. Obviously the Stardust Special had been special in ways he couldn't imagine. He told Mom he was going to the park.

In no time at all he was sitting on the wall outside Old Rosa's house. He didn't know what he was going to say or do, but something inside was telling him if he just confessed, everything would go back to normal.

"Well, well, well," said a voice, and Old Rosa was standing in front of him. "So it's you who's come to see me. What is your name?"

He got to his feet. "William."

"My oh my, William...you never know what each day holds in store, do you?" She scowled and began walking back to her front door. "Well, are you coming?"

He quickly followed her inside and through the house to a small kitchen. "Sit," she told him, pointing to a wooden table and chair in the middle of the floor. "What have you got to say for yourself?"

"I'm sorry for stealing from you," he said, slipping sheepishly into the chair.

Silence for a moment, then her brow furrowed so much it looked like a cheese-grate. "Is that all?"

"I...I think....My...I can't taste...since I ate the...." It took him a moment to recall the name. "...Stardust Special...."

"You thought you would get away with it forever, hmmm? Did you think I would never find out?"

He felt ill.

"*ANSWER ME!*" she roared, her voice booming through the small kitchen.

"I just...I didn't have the money and it looked so...I just had to have it...."

"And how many more...hmm? Did you take something every time? Have you any idea how many children drooled over that basket...kids who would sell a finger for ten dollars just to have one? And do you have any idea how many Stardust Specials were missing by evening time? One, Little William. Just the one." Her face leaned down towards his...her skin hard, fleshy concrete...her eyes dark-green ice. "Each sucker is made by my own hand, the recipe passed down through generations. Heritage. *Tradition!* The worst thing you can steal is a family's tradition, Little William. Wars have been fought over such things."

The idea of a war over stolen suckers should have been funny, but all the laughter had been sapped out of him.

"Understand, William – were you to speak of this to anyone they would find no harmful ingredients here, and no doctor would find anything wrong with you." She smiled. "My family also has recipes which aren't so sweet...but I think you already know that."

When he could speak, his breath was labored. "How long will it last, this...curse?" For that was what it was...a curse. What better word?

"Until you have righted this injustice."

"I'll pay you back!" he cried. "I'll get a paper-route –"

She cackled heartily, head thrown back and her whole body shaking. "You offer me money?" A brisk shake of the head.

"Then please...what can I do?"

She sighed. "If you are really sorry, then the solution is right here in this house. But the question is, are you sorry enough?"

"Yes! I am!"

"Very well." She placed a large white soup-bowl in front of him...it looked old...cracks running through it and a chip out of its rim. It was bigger than any Mom had at home. There was a large spoon with it. "Everything you eat will have bad taste. So you must eat away that bad taste itself!" She left the room, and when she returned she was holding a metal pot with a lid on, and already he could get the stench. When she removed the lid, the stink filled the kitchen and made his stomach knot inside him. She upended the pot and emptied the Brussels Sprouts into the bowl, filling it almost to the top.

Through the rising steam he could see the vegetables...maybe not rotten...but soggy, and burnt to a dark brown. The sharp stink was unfathomable...an acrid stench like needles poking the inside of his nose and making his eyes water. This was how the pizza, and everything else, had been tasting.

He stared at the plate, a lump rising into his throat. "I...I can't...." he stammered.

"No? But it is just a bowl of vegetables."

A loud belch escaped him, and Old Rosa laughed. "Tell me, do you like porridge?"

"Well, yes...it's all right...." Sometimes in the winter Dad would make a pot, and with sugar and strawberry jam on top, it was nice.

"That is fortunate for you, then." She walked to the fridge and William breathed a sigh of relief. The porridge wouldn't be like Dad used to make it but however bad it was, it would still be much better than the sprouts. He was being given a chance.

Old Rosa came back with a plastic mixing-bowl from the fridge, vigorously stirring the contents with a wooden spoon. To his astonishment, she tipped the cold porridge – a gray, thick mulch filled with hard lumps – right into his bowl, on top of the sprouts.

He pushed his chair back from the table and stared in horror as she scraped the gray paste into the bowl. It covered the sprouts, with some of its own lumps out-sizing the vegetables themselves. His mind tried to imagine biting into one of them, and...he slapped a hand to his mouth....

Old Rosa frowned at him as though he were mad. "You don't like? You are lucky – for stealing in my country they would cut off your hand!" She laughed. "Eat it or not...it is your choice."

He reached for the spoon.

Weeks passed while he sat there, staring at the bowl.

Of course, in reality it had only been an hour or so. The porridge was congealing over the sprouts and forming a thick, gray skin atop the bowl. The thought of spooning one of those gray lumps into his mouth made him gag...the idea of chewing one of those burned, porridge-soaked sprouts....

Old Rosa wandered in and out of the kitchen, going about her daily business. "You look pale. You must eat, but you don't want to get sick...believe me, it will taste even worse if the same spoonful has to go down a second time." With a loud cackling she cried, "Eat! Eat!"

He reached with the spoon and scooped up some of the mess; it made a squelchy, sucking sound and one of the sprouts was balanced on the spoon, covered in the vile porridge...he brought it to his mouth with a shaking hand. The stink assaulted his nose; he clenched his teeth and tried not to look at the flap of gray skin dangling down.

His lips parted and he began to tilt the goop onto his tong–

No! He couldn't do it. He slammed the spoon down onto the table and cried.

He left his seat four times...on each occasion getting closer and closer to the door.

Hours passed and he watched the light grow dim through the kitchen window. Evening was falling. Mom would be wondering why he hadn't shown up all day.

Eventually he reasoned...he could sit here into the night, staring at the bowl, or he could close his eyes and spoon the goop into his mouth. Just try and ignore the taste. Try and ignore the texture.

And before he could think himself out of it he grabbed the spoon, filled it, and shoveled it in, his eyes squeezed tightly shut. An explosion of revolting, horrible filth went off inside his mouth with a blast...worse than he could have imagined, but he clamped his lips tight around it and chewed the soft, soggy mouthful until he could squeeze it down his throat. Every muscle in his body was clenching, and he had to grip the edge of the table with one hand to keep from slipping off his chair.

He closed his mind off from the taste. His stomach rose up in revolt, but he ignored its tantrum and forced the mouthful down. Then, before he had a chance to even think about it, the next spoonful went in. Then the next. Then the next.

He'd thought it would get easier with each bite, but it didn't. It got worse. The heavy-salted taste of the porridge intensified and the thick goo lined his gums and tongue, got between his teeth and stuck to the roof of his mouth like a dry paste. His stomach kept trying to throw the disgusting food back up, but he just kept forcing more in. More and more on top of more.

The sound of the spoon scraping the bottom of the bowl was the most wonderful sound he'd ever heard in his life. There were only two sprouts left now in a thin gray soup and he forced them down. His whole body felt weak, and he leaned over to vomit, but he remembered what Old Rosa had said earlier about how it would taste going down for the second time and he somehow forced himself not to throw up.

The door opened and she came in, a huge grin on her face. He stood and walked from the table. He'd never been through anything so horrible in his life. He would never complain about anything his mom ever cooked again! Old Rosa watched in silence until he reached the door. Then she said, "You're leaving so soon, then? Well, until tomorrow...."

He looked back at her. Did she really think he'd be buying any more suckers from her? He couldn't even speak so he shook his head.

"Oh yes. Did you think this was the end of it?" She laughed. "You must return."

"No," he said. "I can't...."

"But you have only eaten one bowl," she cried. "You think that is enough to undo this thing?"

William felt his face sag. "How many...? How many bowls...?" He wanted to get outside, drink fresh air into his lungs.

Her grin widened. "How many?" she echoed. "Well, how many times have you stolen my treats? A bowl for every one, William. A bowl for every single time." Old Rosa laughed, and William thought of all the suckers he'd slipped into his pockets in the last few years. He burst out crying, and allowed Rosa to lead him back to the table.

-end-

More About "Sucker" & Philip Robinson

The morals in "Sucker" are some of the most basic ones we live by. Stealing Is Wrong. Do Not Take Advantage Of People Who Trust You.

I wrote about stealing to illustrate that eventually all thieves get discovered, and sooner or later must answer for their behavior. Stealing leads to lying, even to people you love, and once it starts thieves must lie further to cover their misdeeds. They ultimately end up in a tangled web of deceit, from which there is no escape except to pay, in one way or another, for what they have stolen.

I was born in Dublin City, Ireland, and lived there most of my life before moving to Canada where I live now with my wife and three stepsons. I love reading and writing, playing music (I'm a rock/blues guitarist).

The inspiration for this story comes partly from a lady in my neighborhood – 'The Sucker Lady', as the local kids call her. She makes her own suckers (which are delicious) and sells them to the children who live nearby. I coupled this idea with memories of being a child in Ireland when every morning my dad would make a big pot of porridge. My brothers and sisters didn't seem to mind, but I could not *stand* it! However, it was breakfast and I had to eat a bowl every morning before I went to school. I would sit at the kitchen table, staring at it in horror for half an hour, and then five minutes before I had to leave for school I would grab the spoon and eat it down as quickly as I could, trying not to taste it, or feel the texture in my mouth.

I loved sweets when I was a child, and I still do (I've had to learn to call it candy, though, now that I live in Canada), and

the idea of having every delicious thing taste rotten and burnt is horrifying, so I knew it would be an effective idea for a story.

"Sucker" is my third professional sale. I have a short story included in the hardcover British anthology *Mysterious Erotic Tales* (O'Meara/Castle), within which I'm proud to be included alongside Bram Stoker, Robert Bloch, Ruth Rendell, Patricia Highsmith, Edgar Allen Poe, and others.

I have written the introduction (in the form of fiction) to an upcoming anthology of comedic Lovecraftian stories, entitled *Hastur Pussycat Kill Kill!* (Vox 13), edited by Michael T. Huyck, Jr. This book will be published in three formats – paperback, hardcover, and special limited edition signed by all contributors.

The Paratroop Bear

by Tracy S. Morris

Jumping off the bed was like jumping into the Grand Canyon.

That's what Sue told the other stuffed animals. The bear stood on the edge, trying to keep her balance. Then she felt that second of freefall before the chute opened, leaving her to drift lazily downward until her paws touched down way below. She had a duty to perform, till the light crept back into the corners and closets with the sunrise.

Every morning, Cory's Mother found Sue lying on the floor; she would scoop her up and put her back on the bed.

"What a good teddy," she would tell Cory. "She protects you from the monsters."

"Even the sock-monster under the bed?" Cory would ask.

"Even the sock-monster."

"Even the vampires behind the door?"

"Yes, those, too." Mother would ruffle Cory's hair.

"What about the Gnark in the closet?"

"Him, too," she'd say with a smile. "Now, it's time to get ready for school."

The other animals offered to help Sue.

"Let me help. I'll get that old Vampire with my horns," Moocius, the stuffed cow, said. "When I'm done with him, he'll be walking sore for weeks."

"You couldn't even reach his ankles with your horns," Sue said. "He'll say boo, and you'll run scared."

"I can take that Gnark on," meowed Cally, the gingham cat. "I'll scratch his eyes out with my claws."

"Monsters feed off fear," Sue said with a sigh. "You won't be so brave when you see a real Gnark. Thank you, but I'll work alone."

She might have gone on working alone forever, if not for that dratted school.

One day, Cory came home frowning.

"Jimmy Peckenpaugh told me that teddy bears were for babies," he said.

"Oh dear," said Mother. "Night lights, too?"

"Night lights, too." Cory nodded. "He said that there wasn't any Gnark in the closet. Just my clothes."

So Mother took Sue off the bed.

"I'll leave her on top of the dresser, just in case," Mother said.

Cory's face twisted into an ugly frown when he saw the

teddy on the dresser. "I don't need Her! Teddy bears are for sissies."

"Just for one night," Mother said. "Just to be sure."

"Okay, but I don't need her. I'm not a sissy." With that, Cory climbed in bed and pulled the covers up.

It was one thing to say you weren't afraid, but facing the dark, without a friend to hold your hand is another matter completely. When the moon shines bright through your window, and there is no night-light to hold monsters at bay, the dark flexes its muscles. It creeps and scuttles and gnashes its teeth.

From the top of the dresser, Sue could see the chair behind Cory's bed turn into a three-fanged snark, with eyes like rotten green eggs, and little-boy catching claws. Cory couldn't see it, but he must have felt its hungry breath against the back of his neck. He cautiously turned toward the snark. The monster ducked behind the bed the moment he looked.

Then Cory's winter scarf became a hairy-tusked snoot. The snoot glided up the footboard, its clammy tongue reaching for his toes. Its hairy body rasped on the wood, making a scratchy-scritch sound. The boy turned again, and the snoot dropped out of sight. Muffled by the closet door, a low howl spilled into the room; the ravening Gnark wanted out.

On the bed, Cory shivered. He sat up, hugging himself tightly as he rocked back and fourth.

"It's all in my head," he whispered. Fear stole his breath, making his voice tiny. "There's no such thing as a Gnark. There's no such thing as a Gnark. There's no such thing as a Gnark."

From within the closet, another howl escaped. This one lasted a long time, before breaking into a low keening whine. In reply, Sue heard a faint chuckle behind the door where the vampire lived. Cory must have heard it, too. He whimpered a little and pulled the covers over his head.

The bear felt torn. On one paw, she had to do something, bearfore the monsters got Cory. On the other paw, he'd sent her away. On the other paw, he would eventually stop bearlieving in monsters, and they would all go away. On the other paw, that vampire sounded hungry. Sue had run out of paws and could only come up with one conclusion. She had a job to do.

She turned to gather her parachute. Gone! The word sat on her fiberfill stomach like a lead weight. Where was it? She looked at the bed. There. Mother had left it hanging on the bedpost, where the snoot now curled. Without the parachute, she couldn't jump. The landing would be unbearable.

"Sue?" Cally called out. "Jump. You've got to help us!"

"I can't," the bear said. "I don't have my chute."

"You're just fiberfill!" Moocius cried. "You won't be hurt! Much."

"Why do I always have to be like Bearuce Lee?" Sue complained as she edged her large bottom over the side of the dresser. With a barbearian yell, she let go of the edge, and hurtled toward the floor. As she landed, she felt her bottom split open, and heard the material back there rip. She bounced a few times, and rolled underneath the bed, leaving stuffing behind her.

"What a landing!" She felt her misshapen bottom. Fiberfill hung out through a small tear. She grabbed pawsfull of it, and stuffed it back in, then patted it back into shape. "There's bits of me everywhere. I need to start eating fewer bearitos. Otherwise, I'm bearly going to fit into my chute." Sibilant laughter echoed around her. She glanced up.

The underside of the bed looked like a desert. Dust bunnies rolled through the thickly blanketed grime like tumbleweeds. The musty air pushed in on her, holding her down.

"Who's there?" Her voice echoed in the darkness. Sounding too loud and too high pitched. Terrified. Her stomach twisted in fear. "I'm not afraid of you." Around her, the chittering laughter resumed. Something was making fun of her. All at once, the noise stopped.

"Who are you?" a voice rasped in her ear. Sue jumped. Started. Turned. Nothing there.

"Who are you?" the voice grated into her ear again.

"Who are you?" she countered. The defiance she wanted to feel didn't reach her voice. The strident laughter echoed again. This time, it sounded more like the scrape of dry beetle carapaces against one another.

"Sue!" Cory's shout echoed down to her. It sounded thick, as if smothered by blankets. She turned on a hind paw and darted out from under the bed.

Topside, the shadows had grown. They writhed. Thick leviathans, like Medusa's wig. One stripped the blankets back. Another wrapped around Cory's leg, pulling him off the bed.

The boy whimpered and grabbed at the blankets while the grimy shadows tugged him toward the open closet.

Sue ran behind him, hooking her paw into the boy's hair. Cally and Moocius jumped down to join her. Paws slid over the rug, burning and abrading where they dug in. Cory's slide toward the closet slowed.

"Mother!" he cried out.

The light down the hall came on, shining around the cracks in the bedroom door.

The door opened. Light spilled around Mother's frame and into the room. It splashed golden across the floor and against the walls, chasing the shadows away. In its wake, the snark turned back into a chair. The snoot became a scarf. The leviathan shadows vanished.

"Young man," Mother's tone rang like iron. "You are supposed to be in bed."

"It got me!" Cory sobbed.

Seeing her cub cry, Mother swept him into her arms and held him until his tears subsided. When at last she tucked him in, she pulled out the night-light again.

"I'm glad I saved this," she said as she plugged it in.

"Mother," Cory's voice sounded contrite. "Can I have Sue back?"

"Of course," Mother said. Then she looked at the bear closer. "How on earth did she get torn?" She shook her head. "Oh well, I guess it doesn't matter. I can repair her in the morning."

Before Sue nestled down in Cory's arms, she made sure that she could reach the parachute. Cory believed in monsters again, so they'd be back.

-end-

More About "The Paratroop Bear" & Tracy S. Morris

In the story Cory decides that he doesn't need Sue, so he has Mother put her away. Later, when he does need her, she isn't there to protect him. Sue makes the same mistakes when she thinks that the other stuffed animals can't help her. When she is up on the dresser, it's their advice that helps her to get down. At the end of the story, she relies on them to help her save Cory.

The moral of the story is that you should stand by your friends, because they are the ones who will stick with you through the tough times.

Tracy S. Morris has been writing fiction since the age of twelve. Her most recent work has appeared in the Flesh and Blood anthology *Octoberland*.

She makes her home in Alma, Arkansas, where she's owned by three dogs. She has too many hobbies to mention. By the time this is published, she'll have probably added a couple more, anyway.

The Thing In the Cabinet

by John M. Lance

"**A**re you sure we should be doing this, Jason?"

"Stop whining, Robby. I didn't invite you to tag along. If you don't want to be here, leave." Jason inserted the key he had 'borrowed' from his father's dresser drawer into the lock on the oak cabinet. Giving it a firm twist, he was rewarded with a soft click and the cabinet door swung open. Jason smiled in satisfaction and inhaled the oily, metallic scent of his father's guns.

"Oooo," said Bobby as he peeked over Jason's shoulder, "that one is like the gun in that old movie dad likes so much."

Though the heavy burgundy drapes of the study made the room dark and gloomy even on a sunny afternoon, there was little mistaking the chrome-plated revolver that Robby was pointing to, or the film that had made it famous.

"Dirty Harry." Jason named the movie.

"Yeah, the one we watched on Saturday. That was neat."

"It was ok," Jason shrugged. He didn't particularly like the Dirty Harry movies. The cars and clothes were funny looking, and the villains were silly. Jason would rather see a movie with karate in it, particularly if the hero got to wield a sword.

"Can I touch it?" Robby asked. Before Jason could reply, Robby lifted the pistol from its hooks. "It's heavy. The bullets must weigh a lot."

Jason snorted, "Daddy doesn't keep any of these loaded. The bullets are upstairs in the safe."

Robby frowned incredulously.

Jason shrugged, "If you don't believe me, take the safety off and pull the trigger." Taking the pistol from Robby, he flicked off the safety and handed it back. "Go on."

Pointing down at the floor and closing one eye, Robby pulled the trigger. *Click.* The barrel rotated into position.

"See? Now you've got five more shots left, just like Dirty Harry," Jason said. He scanned the gun case, but all he saw were two rifles and another, older pistol that looked like it came right out a western. Jason frowned; he had been so certain that the samurai sword would be here. Since his father had shown him the sword three weeks ago, Jason had systematically searched the entire house, including the attic and basement, but he never found it. The gun cabinet had been the only place left. As Jason surveyed the cabinet with one last, disappointed look, he noticed a thin shelf at the very top of the cabinet, high out of reach.

Rolling his father's desk chair over to the cabinet, Jason braced it against the door, but when he tried to climb onto it, the chair swiveled and wiggled so much that he nearly fell off. "Robby, hold the chair so I don't tip over."

"Why should I?" Robby asked as he took aim at a pretend bad guy lurking just out of sight. *Click.*

"Because I'm bigger and older than you, and I said so," Jason replied in his most threatening big brother tone.

"Fine," Robby said, taking a firm grasp on the chair back.

Jason climbed up and, after a brief wobble, steadied himself and began feeling around the top shelf. He still wasn't high enough to see, but he could reach all the way to the rear of the shelf. Thick clouds of dust rose as he searched the shelf, and he sneezed twice. Suddenly, his fingertips touched something furry. Patting the mound, he felt a short snout and then felt something cool and sharp. A mischievous grin crept onto Jason's face.

Below him he heard Robby playing. "Take that," *Click,* "and that," *Click.*

"Hey Robby."

"What?"

"Catch," Jason dropped the fox pelt on his brother's head.

"Aaagh!" cried Robby. Throwing the fox fur to the floor, he pointed the pistol at it.

Click.

Jason laughed. Robby pointed the pistol at his brother's chest.

Click.

Jason laughed again. "Looks like you have to reload."
Click.

"See?" Jason giggled again as he renewed his search.

Robby threw the fox fur away from him. "That wasn't funny, Jason." Robby nudged the fox with his toe. "Did Dad shoot it?"

"Yep, a long time ago," Jason replied absentmindedly, "Mom wanted him to throw it out, but he wouldn't so she made him keep it in here." He was just about to give up when his hands came in contact with a cool metallic handle in the farthest corner of the shelf. "Finally," he muttered, but what he drew out of the cabinet wasn't the sword.

"Cool, it's Aladdin's lamp. Well, sort of," Robby said.

Jason had to admit, the oil lamp he held looked exactly like the one he would imagine Aladdin owned, except that it was a dull, almost black silver rather than gold, and he doubted Aladdin's lamp smelled like burnt eggs.

"Rub it and get the Genie to grant you three wishes," Robby said.

Jason decided to humor his brother. "You mean like this?" He rubbed his hand along the lamp's snout with three long, exaggerated sweeps. Instantly, the air in the study grew cold, and Jason and Robby's breaths both rose from their mouths in steamy clouds. Jason shivered.

"So, have you finally decided upon your final wish?" a voice asked from the darkest, most shadowed corner of the room. The old man who stood there was swathed in a red robe that twisted and swirled about him like a python wrapping its coils around its prey. His pallid skin was nearly translucent, and Jason could see blue veins pulsing along the backs of his hands. But it was the man's wrinkled face that fascinated Jason; the old man looked almost exactly like his father, or what Jason imagined his father would look like if he lived to be a hundred years old.

"Eeek!" squeaked Robby. *Click.*

The old man appeared slightly confused. "Neither of you are William Cauldron," he stated.

"He's my father," Jason replied. He knew he should call for his mother and father, yet he found himself intrigued by the old man. And Robby was too frightened to do or say anything. "Who are you?"

The old man ignored Jason's question, posing one of his own instead. "You are the one that rubbed the lamp?"

Jason nodded.

"Then I am now yours to command, young master." The old man bowed deeply, and when he looked up, Jason had the disquieting sense that he was looking in the mirror at an ancient version of himself. "What three wishes may I grant you?"

"A genie!" Robby cried, his fear forgotten.

"Jinn!" the man hissed.

"What?" asked Jason.

"Genies are blue cartoons, figments of an addled brain. I am a jinn, an all-powerful being. It would be best you not forget it; I do not like to repeat myself."

"Yes sir." Robby cowered under the jinn's baleful gaze.

"Wait a minute, you served my father?" asked Jason.

"Yes, yes, faithfully for years, decades in fact. But that is all in the past. Now I serve you."

"But you said he had one wish left."

"Not any more. Any wishes that are not used when a new master summons me are lost. Your father simply waited too long – a mistake I suggest you avoid making yourself."

"But he'll be mad."

"Tut, tut, he did quite alright for himself, I assure you. This beautiful house, his successful business, I gave him all those things. However," the jinn's eyes narrowed, "if you are that concerned, you could wish that he not be mad at you. I could take care of that. I could even make it so that he was happy you took his wish. Whatever you desire."

"Oh, Jason, don't waste your wish on that, wish for a million dollars instead," Robby suggested.

"Why? Mom and dad have plenty of money."

"Or wish for a new bike."

"I have a . . ."

But Robby wasn't listening, "Oh, I know, wish for a million candy bars, or a million wishes, or maybe you can wish that Maryanne from the bus liked you." Robby made kissy noises.

"Maybe I'll wish that you shut up!" Jason snapped.

"Mmmmph!" shrieked Robby. He waved the pistol over his head as he clasped his hand to his mouth.

"What's the matter? Let me see." Jason yanked Robby's hand away. Where his brother's mouth had once been there was now only smooth skin between Robby's nose and chin.

"And what will your second wish be, master?"

"What did you do!" Jason shouted at the jinn.

The jinn frowned. "Granted your wish, of course. You wished that the pest be silent, so I silenced him."

"But his mouth is gone!" Jason cried.

"I fail to see the problem."

"Put it back!"

"Really, you must be more decisive than this. If you really want your brother to have his mouth back, you know what is necessary."

"Fine, fine, I wish that Robby had his mouth back."

"Waaaa," Robby sobbed.

"Robby, are you ok?" Jason knelt down to try to comfort his brother, but Robby pushed him away.

"I'm telling mom you took away my mouth," Robby howled, "and I'm telling Dad you stole his last wish."

"I did not," Jason shouted.

"You did. I wish you never found that lamp."

"Come-on, stop crying," Jason tried to soothe Robby. "We still have one wish left. What do you want to wish for?"

But Robby would not be consoled. He started toward the door, continuing to sob and waving the gun wildly. "I wish that you weren't my brother. I wish that you would just disappear. I wish that I was an only child." Robby stumbled out into the hall.

"Oh yeah," yelled Jason. "Well, I wish I was an only child, too!"

Bang.

"And that," said the jinn, "is that."

Jason stared at the door that Robby had just exited. There were no sounds from the hallway beyond. "What . . . what just happened?" But he knew the jinn's reply even before he heard it.

"I granted your third wish. You are now an only child," said the jinn. The jinn's face had grown fuzzy, and Jason realized that he could see through the old man to the wall behind him.

"Where are you going? You have to fix this."

"I've fulfilled my service to you, now my lamp and I will depart until someone else discovers us and begins the cycle anew."

The lamp felt lighter, and when Jason looked down he could see the outline of his palms through the metal. "Wait! I'll give the lamp to my mother. She can wish this never happened."

The hazy outline of the jinn smiled an evil smile, "Silly boy, if that were allowed to happen the lamp would simply be handed from person to person until everyone in the world had all of their wishes come true. That would not stand. After all, this is real life, not some fairy story."

"I wish it was a fairy tale," Jason said as the last smoky vestiges of the lamp disappeared.

"Of course you do. After all, fairy tales end, but a bullet, well..." the disembodied voice gave a final, nasty snicker, "...a bullet is forever."

-end-

On "The Thing In the Cabinet" & John M. Lance

When pointing out morals, you always have to be wary of climbing up on your own personal soapbox and shouting too loudly, lest your message be dismissed as the ravings of a lunatic with just a little too much free time on his/her hands. Therefore, I will keep this brief. The morals of "The Thing In the Cabinet" are:

- Be careful what you wish for, you just might get it – this moral is actually more an object lesson in the avoidance of guilt than anything else since, in the end, few people can cause bad things to happen simply by wishing they were so. Still, if you want to be karmicly sound and, more importantly, able to sleep at night, it is always best to avoid wishing ill on others.

- Don't play with guns – one of those morals you would hope would not have to be repeated, but then, sometimes even the obvious bears repeating – Don't play with guns. They are not toys, but rather highly effective tools whose intent is to kill things. I do not know who said it first, but I firmly believe in the saying, "Never point a gun at anything unless you intend to destroy it."

I live in the American North East with my lovely wife, Deb, beautiful daughter Morgan, and two Labrador Retrievers, Hershey and Cadbury. My publishing credits include "Bobby's Troll" – Spellbound Magazine: Summer 2001, "The Field Trip" – Spellbound Magazine: Fall 2001, and "The Attack of the Blueberry Beast" – Spellbound Magazine: Spring 2002.

Hey Laura!
Enjoy!

SHHHHH!

by Laura J. Underwood

Laura Underwood

Once upon a time, in a cozy brick townhouse in the suburbs of a great big city, there lived a little girl named Katie Chatterbox. Her real name was Katie Lebowitz, and she was as pretty and smart and sweet a child as anyone could ask for. Except for one bad habit.

Katie would not shut up.

Nope, not for one minute. Not even when her mother begged her and her father shouted at her. Why even when she got spanked for running her mouth off at inappropriate times (which was nearly all the time she wasn't sleeping), she would wail and whimper and rattle off all the promises in the world to be a good little girl and generally devote ten minutes to the apology.

It was enough to turn a saint to sin. Many of the folk who had lived on their street had either installed extra insulation on their walls to deaden the sound or moved to other neighborhoods. Their children were forbidden to play with Katie for fear they would start talking like she did. And as for her teachers... Katie spent a lot of time in the Principal's office. So much so, the Principal was threatening suicide.

Over time, this drove her father to stay late at his accounting office, and her mother took to drinking and popping various pills to dull the sound. Katie, of course, did not seem to notice that her parents were losing interest in her continual attempts at conversation. She rattled on merrily day in and day out. Saying much without saying anything at all.

One day, in a fit of nurturing—or perhaps just seeking a sanctuary of silence—Katie's mother decided to visit the public library. Now, libraries have changed a lot over the years. They don't just have musty old books. In fact, this library was a state of the art center of information. There were computer terminals with access to the Internet (though some people complained that these were being used by local perverts who liked to peruse porn on them), and Books on Tape that could either be listened to on a home cassette player or on the library headsets. One could view the latest videos and check out the latest music CDs. In other

words, there were lots of ways to occupy oneself that involved
headphones so one did not have to listen to a chattering child.

"Now, you have to be quiet in the library, Katie," Mother
said as they rode downtown on the subway.

"Why?" Katie asked. This was, after all, her first visit to
the heart of the great big city.

"Because that's the rule," Mother said. "Libraries are
places of silence, and the Librarian will shush you if you make
noise."

"Okay," Katie said, though she had no idea what it meant
to be shushed. "If it's the rule, I will be as quiet as a mouse.
Except mice aren't really quiet, you know. They chew on the
walls and the insulation and the wiring, and I hear them running
around in the walls and chittering all the time. Or am I hearing
rats? Daddy says there are rats in the walls, and they make all
kinds of noises..."

Mother popped a Valium and downed it with a swig from
the vial of emergency gin in her purse. Then she stared at the
passing lights in the subway tunnel while Katie nattered on.

It took longer than usual to get downtown, probably
because Katie's incessant yammering caused half the passengers
in the train car to disembark well before they reached their stops.
In fact, the only person left in the car was the wino who refused
to share his bottle of cheap muscatel with Katie's mother. But at
last, they reached the downtown station. Even the wino looked
rather relieved when Katie and her mother left the train.

Katie, of course, was in heaven. "What's that big
building? Can we go up there? Do they have a swimming pool?
Can I go swimming?" Mother alternately answered with "yes,"
"no," and "will you please shut up!" for all the good it served.
"You have to be quiet in the library, Katie. Bad things happen to
children who are not quiet in the library. Why, I have heard that
the librarian will eat you if you're not quiet!"

"Eat me?" Katie asked.

"Yes," Mother said and her eyes darted nervously
towards the doors. "When I was a little girl, I came here with my
friend Sarah, and she wouldn't be quiet either, and the librarian
became so angry, she ate Sarah."

"Why?"

"Because some people say she is really a troll," Mother
replied.

"That's silly," Katie said. "There are no trolls. Besides,
if she eats me, she'll just get indigestion. Daddy said I would
give indigestion to a troll..." Katie continued this aimless

chattering so that by the time they reached the doors of the library, Mother was clamping a hand firmly over Katie's mouth and glaring into her beloved daughter's wide eyes.

"Shut up, damn you!" Mother ordered with a certain amount of irrational hysteria in her voice, and it quelled Katie for all of a moment. At least long enough for them to get inside and Mother to head for the nearest enclosed carrel. In fact, she was gone so fast, Katie found herself standing alone in a vast room in which a bare whisper could be heard like a breeze among the tree leaves. Not that Katie would know what the whisper of a breeze sounded like, as she had never been quiet long enough to hear such a peaceful sound.

Katie looked up and spied a high dome ceiling that had been painted in the manner of Michaelangelo's Sistine Chapel, only this was a rendition of an ancient Greek library. However, Katie knew nothing of Michael Angelo or Greeks, and she certainly didn't know that she was seeing a group of people in togas listening to an elderly scholar.

"Wow, look at that!" she said aloud, pointing a chubby finger at the long tubes of rolled paper that lined the painted shelves in the illustration. "Why are those people wearing bed sheets?"

"Shhhhh!"

Katie turned. Behind the desk was the librarian. Quite a lot of librarian, in fact. She was a rather large, bulky woman with a strange greenish cast to her skin. She made one think of mountains and moss and granite, and her eyes were dark as holes in the ground. Ugly too. She reminded Katie of a picture in some old fairytale book she had. The librarian glowered at Katie over the tops of her spectacles.

With a shrug, Katie turned back to her perusal of the painting, turning in a circle in the center of the room. The men and women were half naked, and several of them held what looked like long skinny rolls of toilet paper. Katie had never seen anything quite like them before. And she wanted to know what they were, so she walked over to the front desk and looked up at the librarian who wore a nametag that said "Miss McTrow." The librarian looked back, still wearing that ugly frown. Boy, did she have a really big mouth too. Sort of like a giant greenish bullfrog. Katie was willing to bet her whole head would fit inside that mouth.

"May I help you?" the librarian asked.

Katie squinted up at the dark eyes and said, "What are those people doing?"

"Which people?" Miss McTrow asked.

Katie gestured up at the ceiling painting. "*Those* people," she said and her voice grew in volume. "Is that toilet paper they're looking at? Because if it is, they must have really big butts to need toilet paper that big..."

"Shhhhh!" Miss McTrow hissed.

"I only wanted to know what they were doing," Katie said with a pout.

"They are reading," Miss McTrow said. "Now you must not talk in here, little girl, because you are disturbing the other patrons...and I'm getting hungry."

"But what are they reading?" Katie protested. "Why would anyone want to read a roll of toilet paper...except my daddy had a roll of toilet paper once that had these weird pictures of naked people that he used to keep hidden in the closet, and one day I..."

"They are reading scrolls," Miss McTrow said in a surly tone. "Does that answer your question?"

"Well, I don't know," Katie said. "What's a scroll?"

The librarian made a sound that resembled a grunting frog's sigh. Still, she turned and waddled along the length of the desk. Katie followed, puzzled by this behavior. Miss McTrow rounded the end of the desk on tree-trunk legs and made her way across the room.

"This way," Miss McTrow said and led Katie over to a glass library case. Inside lay what looked like unfurled rolls of toilet paper — or maybe it was paper towels — but there were sticks on each end that looked like old rolling pins, and across the surface were weird letters and symbols.

"This is a scroll," Miss McTrow said. "This is how our ancient ancestors recorded history and stories, by hand before they learned how to bind books. Does that answer your question?"

Katie was too busy staring at the scroll to notice when Miss McTrow lumbered quietly back to her post behind the main desk. "Wow, so that's a scroll?" Katie leaned this way and that. "How can anyone read it? Boy I bet they got an F in handwriting 'cause that don't look like words..." No matter what angle she achieved, the face of the scroll remained the same. "How do you open this thing? I want to hold it." Katie tried to crawl under the case, but there was a wooden base in her way. So on desperation, Katie tried to climb up above the case, but the surface was too slick to afford her any purchase. She slid off with a loud squeal of skin on glass and landed on the floor in a heap. "Ouch!"

she screamed.

"Shhhhhhhh!" Miss McTrow hissed again, and there was a slither of spittle at the corner of her mouth.

Katie made a face. "Did you just fart?" she asked as she clambered to her feet. Rubbing her butt, she approached the desk once more. "Because it sure sounds like you farted. My mother always sounds like that when she farts, but then my Daddy says my Mother's farts are silent but deadly, while his are so loud they echo, and Mother says he's going to vibrate all the windows in the neighborhood..."

"Shhhhhh!" Miss McTrow's frown actually increased. And her mouth looked a little wider. In fact, she seemed to be puffing up like some enormous toad. "Be quiet. You're making me hungry, little girl."

But Katie was on a roll. "I don't fart," she said. "Not where anyone can hear me, but once I went into the closet and farted to see if I could make it sound real loud, and Mother got mad because she said I made the whole bedroom stink like a dirty sock..."

Miss McTrow leaned over the counter and seized Katie by the arm. She lifted Katie right off the ground, and Katie squealed as though she had been gutted.

"Shhhhhhhhh!" Miss McTrow hissed. "You are breaking the rules, little girl. No loud talking in the library! Am I going to have to eat you to make you be quiet?"

Several people were now stirring, most of them making quiet exits from the room.

"But that's a silly rule," Katie said. "How can people ask you questions if they don't talk?"

"Shhhhhhhhhhhhhhhh!" Miss McTrow gave Katie a shake, and then dropped her to the floor. "Shhhhhhhhhhh!" The librarian's head began to swell so that her mouth spread twice as wide as before. "Shhhhhhhhhhhhh!" The hiss of her voice sounded more like she was slobbering.

Katie stood there with her mouth gaped in wonder, silent for the first time in years. It looked like Miss McTrow was going to burst, she was growing so big. Around her, the remaining people were leaping out of chairs and carrels and making for the doors. Some of the other librarians hastened through other exits. It was as if no one wanted to be around to see what was about to happen.

"Oh, wow!" Katie said and started to back away.

But before she could take another step, Miss McTrow opened her mouth real wide. Katie could see rows upon rows of teeth

and a long tongue. The latter suddenly lashed out at Katie like a whip. Before she could duck or raise her hands, it wrapped around her ankles and yanked her upside down into the air. She found herself dangling over the large mouth.

"Didn't I warn you that if you didn't shut up, I would eat you?" Ms. McTrow said. Her skin was turning green and warty.

"Ewwww, your breath stinks!" Katie declared.

But that was all she said. For suddenly, she was dragged into that massive maw, slipping and sliding down the throat that closed around her. She couldn't even scream as she sank into a slimy, smelly dark. With one great gulp, Miss McTrow swallowed Katie whole.

Katie slid down into a stomach, bile filling her throat and lungs. And just before all awareness faded, she heard Mother's voice sounding very far away.

"Oh, Katie, I told you that you had to be quiet in the library..."

-end-

More About "Shhhhh!" & Laura J. Underwood

The moral of this story. There are several, actually. Silence is golden, but even more so, if your parents tell you to be quiet, maybe you should listen to them. Sometimes, we can avert danger simply by being quiet and listening....

What inspired me to write this story? I am a librarian who spends part of her time trying to convince people that computers will not eat them and that bound books are still useful.... Frequently, I meet children whom I sometimes wish had an "off" button — my own niece comes to mind. The others who inspired it shall remain nameless. This is not to say that I object to children being themselves. But rather, I find myself wishing there was a way to convince them to be quiet.

And while I do not resemble the librarian in this tale, be warned. If I put my fingers to my lips and tell you, "Shhhhh!" it would probably be a good thing to listen.

Laura J. Underwood has published over fifty short stories in magazine and anthologies. Her tales have appeared in various volumes of *Sword and Sorceress* and *Marion Zimmer Bradley's Fantasy Magazine* as well as *Bubbas of the Apocalypse* and *Such A Pretty Face*. Additionally, she is the author of two novels, *Ard Magister* (from Yard Dog Press) and *The Black Hunter*, and two collections of short fiction. When not writing, she is a librarian, a harpist and a fencer with the SFWA Musketeers.

GUNTHER'S GRUBBYS
by Jax Laffer

"**Y**ou stupid old man! Gimme my tickets!" Butch shouted, his face a valentine red. He was standing outside the now locked doors of Gunther's, watching the janitor, Mr. Cravetts, sneer at him from inside. Me and Dooley, that's Butch's little brother, and Sam, short for Samantha, were all watching a very angry Butch kick at the glass doors.

Oh, by the way, I'm Eddie.

"I spent my whole allowance in that dumb place!" Butch yelled. He turned and walked into the parking lot, stomping his feet. He did that well. No one could stomp their feet like Butch. It showed the whole world how he felt.

"C'mon, Butch. I'm sure we can talk to the owners tomorrow and they'll give you the tickets." Sam was always the cheerleader. She tried to make him feel better, but that was a "no way," *major*!

"That's not the first time he's kept my tickets! Why does a dumb old man who hates kids work in a place like Gunther's anyway?" Butch asked the sky. He must have gazed at the clouds for a whole thirty seconds before he calmed down.

"You mean he's done this before?" asked Dooley with wide eyes.

"Course he has! He loves making us kids mad. He loves taking our money then throwing us outta there with nothing to show for it. And I only needed three hundred and two more tickets before I could get that Star Power Ranger set behind the counter!"

"How many tickets did you have this time, Butch?" I asked, getting ready to duck. He was still angry enough to thwap me on my head if he had a mind to.

"Three hundred and twenty nine!" Butch said, getting mad all over again. "That stupid Ranger set was seventeen hundred and fifty tickets altogether! Today, I had enough to finally take it home! Now I'm broke and won't have any money again for a week, and it'll be gone by then, *major*!"

"*Minor*, Butch," I said. "You can have my tickets." I pulled them out of my pocket and handed them to him.

A smile crossed his face, finally. "How many you got here, Eddie?"

"Well, uh, only about fifty-eight, but you can have them all."

"Oh, man, that ain't near enough!" he said, then tossed them to the ground.

I gathered them up as Butch, Dooley and Sam started to head for home. I don't think I ever saw Butch so upset.

Just as we rounded the corner, Butch had one of his brilliant ideas. He stopped and looked at the sky again. I knew trouble was brewing. I didn't like the look on his face even if it was a sorta happy kinda look.

"I just got a brilliant idea!" he said.

Course he did. Didn't I tell ya?

"This is what we're gonna do!"

We all huddled together like a football team at the fifty-yard line, arms around each others shoulders, looking down at the ground.

"Tonight," he began, "just when everyone is asleep, we'll sneak out and go get my tickets. Then we'll leave, and go back tomorrow and get my Ranger set!"

Sam looked up startled. "But Butch, we can't break in Gunther's like that! We could go to jail!" she shouted.

"Shhhhhh! Shhh!" Spit flew from Butch's mouth. "Will you keep quiet? You wanna get us caught before we even *do* anything?"

"Uh, Butch," Dooley said a bit scared. "But what if we *do* get caught?"

"Yeah, Butch. We could be in trouble, *major*!" I said, waiting to hear thunder come out of Butch's mouth.

Instead, Butch just smiled. He huddled us together again. "Now, listen. Tonight at midnight, we'll sneak out of our houses, meet right here behind those bushes."

"Just how we gonna get in, anyway?" I asked him. "Gunther's probably has an alarm system set up. Cops will be there before we get through the front door."

"Naw, man," Butch said. "Cravetts don't leave there until after midnight. That's when his shift is over. He usually stays to eat the last of the garbage stuff the kids didn't finish at dinner. Alls we gotta do is sneak in the back door before he leaves. It's a no brainer, *minor*!"

"I dunno, Butchy. Mom and Dad will be awful mad if they find out," Dooley said.

"They won't find out, and don't call me Butchy!" Butchy

- I mean *Butch* said.

"Well, suppose you can't find your tickets?" Sam was always asking the hard questions.

"I know exactly where old man Cravetts keeps them. In a drawer behind the counter. It's down by the floor. It's his own personal drawer with all his own stuff in it. Kinda like a locker," Butch said.

"Yeah, but is it locked?" I had to ask.

"No, it ain't locked!" Butch sounded mad again.

"Well, how do you know all this stuff? I mean, about when Cravetts leaves, and if his drawer is locked, and, well, and uh, even what he eats there late at night?" Sam was almost gonna get thwaped, I could feel it.

Butch looked at her. "Because, *Samantha,* my older sister used to work there at night before she got outta school. That's how. She's the one who got them to put macaroni and cheese on the menu."

"Oh."

"Now, are we on for tonight, or are we gonna be like itty bitty babies and just let old man Cravetts get the better of us?" Butch looked like if any of us said no, he would kill us.

After we stood there a second or two, pondering all that could happen to us with our folks if we got caught, we did a dumb thing. We agreed.

By my Space Ranger alarm clock, it was eleven fifty-nine. I was gonna be late. I knew they'd wait for me though. As soon as I dared, I got out of bed and dressed. My window opened with a creak, but I climbed out onto the roof and went to the big pine tree. I had climbed down this tree hundreds of times but never in the dark.

When I reached the street corner no one was there. At first I thought they all gave up and decided not to break into Gunther's Grubbys. But then I heard a real bad imitation of a meadowlark coming from under the bushes and knew they were there. I sneaked through that bush on my hands and knees, and got several scratches on my face.

"Man, Butch, couldn't you think of a better place to meet than this?" I asked, rubbing my chin. When I looked, Butch, Dooley and even Sam all had scratches on their faces. No one said a word.

We got up and quietly walked down the street toward Gunther's. This was a small town, Fallen Rock was. We had no streetlights and of course, there was no moon tonight. No one noticed us.

Butch finally broke the silence. "I only hope that old man is still there swiping food!"

It was almost twelve-thirty when we arrived at the back of Gunther's Grubbys Fun Palace. It was so dark we couldn't even see the door. We had to feel our way around the alley with our hands just hoping to come across a doorknob. I never thought a dumb old stray cat could scare me, but when one jumped out at us from the trash bin, I thought I'd wet my pants.

As we all caught our breath, we heard a doorknob turn right in front of us. We scrambled to hide behind the trash bin, sweatin' like pigs at the slaughterhouse. Cravetts came out with his back to us, carrying two large boxes of trash. We almost laughed out loud watching the old man. He had to stretch his body in a real awkward way to keep a foot in the door for the light to shine through, and open the trash bin lid. He almost fell down throwing the boxes inside, but he caught the lid just as it was slamming down. He turned and started back inside, then suddenly stopped. He must have heard Dooley snicker. We all held each other's mouth shut with our hands.

Cravetts turned his head, looked around the alley, then shrugged his shoulders and went back inside. We were safe.

We waited for a minute, then Butch rose and went to the door. He carefully turned the knob and it creaked. He stopped dead still, listening for any sign of Cravetts. Nothing. He motioned for us to get up.

We followed Butch into Gunther's and found ourselves in the kitchen. We'd never been back here before. This was where all the great food was made. Pizza, PB and J, macaroni and cheese, chicken fingers and fries, all the stuff kids like, plus the ice cream counter and pastry shelf. None of that adult stuff like chef salads, steaks, seafood and junk. This was strictly a kids store.

Dooley looked at the back of the ice cream counter, then tugged on Butch's shirttail.

"What!" Butch snapped in a whisper.

"Uh, I'm gettin' kinda hungry, Butchy," Dooley said, never taking his eyes off the ice cream.

"Not now, you dumbhead," Butch whispered. "We gots work to do!"

The lights started to go out. First in the first dining room where all the games were, like Basketball, Air hockey, Whack-a-mole, Spider Stomp, Skee Ball and the big tube-type jungle gym play area. This was where Butch had won all his tickets.

Then, lights punched out in the main dining room where the Grubbys Fun Palace Band was on a stage. There were about

forty tables for birthday parties there, and Gunther and his band
of electronic animals played instruments and mechanically sang
songs to entertain the crowds.

We heard a whistling sound, much like something coming
outta someone's mouth with no teeth, coming outta the bathroom.
We glanced at each other and tried our best to find a place to
hide. Cravetts was coming.

Sam and I hid behind some cabinets in the corner of the
kitchen, and stupid, dumb Butch and his brother ran into the
walk-in freezer and shut the door.

Cravetts came walking into the kitchen turning off more
lights. He was getting ready to leave. Soon, all the lights in the
place were out and Cravetts went out the back door. Sam and I
heard the key turn in the lock.

Sam started breathing hard and we waited to make sure
Cravetts was gone. Then we jumped up and ran to the freezer.
Butch was looking out the small window on the door, mouthing
some kinda words we couldn't hear. He looked scared to death.
And cold.

Sam and I tried to get the door open, but we couldn't
budge it. I looked up at Butch and saw him pointing to the left. I
couldn't make out what he was trying to tell us. Alls I knew was
we had to get them outta there, and fast ... *major!*

Butch looked like he was gonna cry. I kept trying to get
the long knob of the freezer door down to open, but there was
just no way. Oh, no. Butchy and Dooley were gonna die frozen,
like a couple of popsicles. Then, Sam suddenly caught on. Butch
was trying to tell us to look to the left.

She left the door and went around the corner. There on
the wall was a key. She grabbed it and quickly unlocked the
freezer door.

Together, we pulled hard and the huge door swung open.
Butch and Dooley came falling out the opening, gasping for air.

"Couldn't you breathe in there?" Sam asked.

"Yeah, we ... breathe ... just ... cold!" Dooley sorta said.

When Butch finally got hold of himself he said, "Man,
couldn't you find the key any faster?"

"I thought you were gonna die in there!" Sam said, near
tears. "I did the best I could! I didn't know what you were trying
to tell us!"

"Sam, you did good, *major!*" I told her and swung an
arm around her shoulder. "You saved their lives! Didn't she ...
Butchy?"

Butch looked at her. "Yeah, I guess I owe ya."

Sam brushed herself off. She was still mad. "Well, let's just get this over with!" She turned to go into the first dining room where the order counter was. We followed.

Surprisingly, the counter was still lit up. Neon signs and colorful flood lights were behind the counter where all the gifts were on shelves. Right there, in the middle of the third shelf up, was the Ranger set Butch wanted. We all stood, gaping up at it.

"Maybe I should just take it and run," Butch said, not taking his eyes from it.

"Dontcha think that'd be stealin'?" Dooley said.

"Stealin'? Doncha think we're already in trouble for being here in the first place?" Butch said to him. Dooley looked down at the floor.

"Yeah, well, don't make matters worse," I told him. "Let's just get the tickets back and get outta here!"

Butch started for Cravetts' drawer. I looked around and saw that Sam was gone.

She had wandered off into the main game room. I followed her instead of staying with Butch.

"Jeez, I always wanted to play this game," she said, eyeing the Spider Stomp.

I came up behind her. "Then why haven't you?"

She looked up at me. And sorta in a question, she said, "Cause, I hate spiders?"

"All the more reason to play the game . . . so you can stomp on 'em!" I told her, grinning.

She put her hand in her jean pocket and pulled out a single token. "Do you think I dare?"

"Why not? No one's here but us spider killers."

Slowly, she put the token in the slot next to where the tickets came out. The more spiders you stomped, the more tickets you got, and the more tickets you got, the bigger the prize you could buy with them.

Suddenly, Butch and Dooley were next to us. "And to think we have this whole place to ourselves tonight!" Butch said, grinning. He held out his hands and showed us a zillion tokens he took from Cravetts' drawer.

"You gotta be kidding me, *major*!" Sam said, her eyes widening.

"Nope, here, some for you, some for us. Now let's have some fun before we leave!" Butch headed for the Space Helicopter, and Dooley went for the tube playground.

I stood there watching as the Gunther Grubby's Fun Palace came to life at one in the morning. All the bells were going off on the games being played and I became afraid that someone might hear us.

Just then, Gunther's Band started to play and sing in the other birthday dining room. We all stopped and looked at each other.

We left the games and walked cautiously into the room. There they were, the band, lights, cameras and television screens, screaming songs to an empty crowd.

Chickidee, the Chicken singing in her animated way into a microphone, Hoody the Hounddog playing the organ, Bee Bop the Bear playing the guitar, and good old Gunther the Gorilla playing the drums. They were six-foot tall mechanical robots, staring at nothing, moving in jerky ways as they strummed, beat, and sang tunes.

Gotta tell ya, it looked pretty scary this late at night with just the four of us in there . . . alone.

"How . . . what made them start playing?" Sam asked, moving close to me and taking my arm.

"Dunno. But I don't think I like it too much," Butch said. He ran fingers through his strawberry blonde hair. "Maybe we should just get the stuff we came for and leave."

"That's a *major* idea, dude, " I told him. We headed back behind the counter in the other dining room to get his tickets.

We were in a single file behind the counter, Butch bending over the drawer, stuffing his pockets with tickets. Sam was next to him trying to hurry him up. I stood there next to Sam and waited. Dooley was pulling on my shirt saying he wanted to go home.

Then it happened. We heard a low growl come from behind Dooley. Butch stood up staring at his ten year old brother. Sam stared at Butch, then slowly turned around to stare at Dooley. I saw Sam's blank eyes, and turned to look at Dooley to ask him why he was growling. But Dooley was looking right at me. That's when I saw him. It was Hoody the Hounddog. He towered over Dooley a good three feet.

Dooley was shaking. He couldn't talk. He knew something was behind him, but there was no way he was going to turn around. Instead he just stared at my openly shocked face.

Hoody's face was no longer that of the kind looking hound dog. It was alive, just as alive as the rest of us. He was moving on his own. Dooley shook hard when he felt huge paws on his shoulders. Those paws pulled him backward and out of the counter area. I thought Dooley was gonna die from fright. He never looked behind him.

Hoody's mouth opened. We saw huge, white pointed teeth, and spit drooling down his chin. A large, red tongue came out and licked his lips. Hoody picked Dooley up and started to stuff him into his large mouth, all the while drooling down his chin. Then, his teeth came together and he started chewing Dooley up like he was a dog bone.

Dooley was gone. Hoody wiped his mouth with a large paw and started to howl. It was so loud, I covered my ears. I heard Sam behind me starting to scream.

Hoody looked at us, then went back to the stage and just stood there. Butch, Sam and I just froze. Somehow, Butch got the nerve to move. He shoved me and Sam outta the way and barreled through the counter, racing toward the stage. "You gimme back my little brother, you . . . you vampire!"

I ran after Butch and caught him before he reached the stage. He fought me to let him go, but I couldn't. "Dooley's gone, Butch. We havta get outta here!"

"I ain't leavin' without my brother!" he yelled. "Now lemme loose!"

I couldn't hang on any longer. I ripped Butch's shirt as he flew up on the stage and started beating Hoody with his fists.

I looked around the stage and saw that Chickadee wasn't there anymore. Now where did that stupid chicken go?

That's when I thought of Samantha. I turned and ran back to the order counter where I left her. She wasn't there. I saw Chickadee. She was walking and there were no plug wires. No cables to make her work. She was moving on her own. She was chanting, "Here chick, chick, chick, come out to play . . ." Then she would cluck. Over and over and over. I had to cover my ears. But, where was Sam?

Chickadee moved from the counter and went into the game room. Still clucking and calling out for someone.

I hid inside the tube playground. Where was Sam? Maybe if I couldn't find her, neither could Chickadee. I could still see the stage; Butch was still beating on Hoody yelling to get his brother back. Hoody stood there motionless.

When I looked back at Chickadee I heard a terrible scream. She had found Sam hiding behind the Skee Ball game. I couldn't believe what I was seeing. Chickadee grabbed Sam off the floor by the neck and started to stuff Sam in her mouth. Alls I could see after that was Sam's legs in a running motion, trying to get spit up by a giant chicken. Then, Sam was gone.

I decided to stay right where I was. No six foot animal was gonna get me in here. I was in the middle of the tube playground and even a large adult could not get up here. These animals were so fat and tall there was no way they could fit in here. Could they?

That's when I heard Butch screaming and running to the game room. Chickadee was now back on the stage, and Butch was yelling for Samantha. He couldn't find her. Then he yelled for me. There was no way I was gonna give my position away. But how was I gonna help Butch if I stayed put? I just knew one of those animated monsters was gonna come after Butch soon, but which one, and when?

Butch was crying. Imagine a twelve-year old boy crying. I couldn't believe it as I wiped tears away from my own twelve-year-old eyes.

Butch ran back to the game room. He looked at the monsters on stage. That's when he saw slimy drool all over Chickadee's mouth and figured out she had gotten one of us.

He turned, and with a face as white as Casper's, he yelled again, "Eddie! Sam! Where are you!"

I couldn't stand it anymore. I had to yell help. "BUTCH! I'M UP HERE! GET IN THE TUBES! HURRY!" I yelled.

I saw Butch freeze at the sound of my voice. Then a relieved sigh escaped his mouth and he headed for the playground. "What's going on here!" he shouted at me as he tried to get up the ladder inside the yellow tube.

"I dunno, but they can't get us up here. They can't fit in the tubes. Hurry up!"

Just as Butch got to the third rung of the ladder, something grabbed his foot. It was Bee Bop. The biggest, hairiest bear I ever saw, with teeth the size of my whole hand, and saliva dripping from his open jowls.

Butch screamed. Bee Bop started eating his foot. First one, then the other. Alls I saw of Butch after that was a horrified look on his face as Bee Bop swallowed him whole. Then, pretty as you please, Bee Bop belched, wiped his mouth and went back to the stage. That only meant one thing. Gunther was the only monster left . . . and he was a gorilla.

I was next. What was I gonna do? Stay in this tube all night? Until the place opened up in the morning? It didn't open until eleven for lunch. I was gonna hafta stay here until then! I had to go to the bathroom.

It was the first day of school. I was gonna miss it. Mom and Dad were gonna wonder where I was. Summer vacation was over, and I wasn't going to be there with all my friends. All my friends? Butch, Sam? Even Dooley. Sure he was two years younger than us, but he was always with us. What would my teacher say? The Principal? WHO CARED? Why was I worrying about school and Mom and Dad and my teacher when I just lost my best friends? Wow! The things a kid thinks about when you are trapped inside a fun palace with real live monsters!

Alls I could think about now was getting outta here. I had to get outta here and tell someone about what's happened. Who was I gonna tell? Who would believe me? They would all think I was making it up, *major*!

I could barely see the clock on the wall over the order counter. It read three o'clock. I still had to go to the bathroom! I looked around and down at the stage. All was quiet there, including Gunther, the Gorilla. Maybe I had to take a chance. I knew he couldn't get me in here. But what was he waiting for? Did he know that, too?

I started to move. Only an inch at a time. I crawled through the pink tube and headed down the end to the big bubble. At least from there I could see the whole restaurant. That way I could keep a close watch on Gunther. He still stood there, dead still. I seemed to make it with no trouble, but boy! Did I have to go to the bathroom! Only a little farther and I'd be outta this dumb, stupid place!

I looked back at the stage and started to smile. But I smiled too soon. Gunther was gone. That's when I was afraid I'd soil my pants, but I didn't. Quickly, I shoved two fingers in my mouth. My dad always told me on road trips in the car, that if I had to go to the bathroom before he found one, to suck on two fingers. It would get my mind off it. Alls that happened this time, was that my two fingers got all wrinkly.

I couldn't see Gunther anywhere, but I knew he was out there. I moved slowly from the bubble and headed across a rope ladder. That's when I saw him. Even though I was ten feet above him, he was the biggest dark blue gorilla I'd ever seen. He was just standing there, looking at me, and waiting.

"I'M NOT COMING DOWN TO YOU . . .YOU . . . BIG APE!"

"Oh, yes you will, sooner or later. Or maybe I'll just send Gunther up to you!" a voice yelled, clear from the kitchen. It was Cravetts. Had he been there all along?

"Cravetts, you old goat! What's going on? Help me!" I shouted.

"Nope. Since youse guys decided to steal from me, you have to pay!"

"We didn't steal from you! You stole tickets from Butch!"

"Then we'll just say . . . it's the best way to keep Gunther Grubby's Fun Palace running. You don't think this great band work for peanuts do you? No. They like to be paid in children. Children who disobey their parents and sneak out of their houses late at night. It's the children that keep this place alive."

I knew he had me. He was right. We did wrong sneaking out. But there was no way Gunther was gonna get me in here. He was too big, and the tubes were too small.

"You better come down, Gunther's getting mighty hungry!"

I laughed a sinister laugh. "Not on your life, you old . . . man!" I knew I was safe, or he wouldn't have told me to come down.

That's where I was wrong. I saw Gunther. This big gorilla shimmered in the neon lights of the order counter. Suddenly, he became almost invisible, almost skinny and a light shade of blue. And with one swoop, he disappeared into the tubing of the playground, grunting all the way. Yep, I felt him grab my leg. I kicked him in the face as hard as I could and got free.

I raced along on my hands and knees to the red tube. That tube was a slide. I knew if I made it to the slide, I could get past Cravetts and get out the back door. I scooted along and turned the wrong way toward the blue tube. That was not the slide I needed. It led to the playhouse full of plastic balls. I backed up. And there was Gunther!

I went toward the tube that led me to the balls and slipped down it. I fell directly into the balls and thought for a minute that I should stay there and just hide in them. That wouldn't work. Gunther knew I was headed that way. Even if the balls covered me completely, he'd know I was there.

I jumped up and waded through all the yellow, blue and red balls to the opening, then pulled myself up and out the hole. Then I heard a thud. It was Gunther, right behind me!

I moved as fast as I could until I finally reached the opening and got out of the tube playground. Now, maybe I was safe. That's when I saw Cravetts. He reached for me, his eyes red and glowing. His mouth in this huge grin showing yellow decayed teeth. I hit him hard in the stomach and raced for the back door.

But, that's when Gunther caught me. He grabbed the back of my neck and turned me around to face him. Alls I saw were these beady little eyes, dark and close together. A black snout with flaring nostrils. An open mouth with lots of sharp, pointed teeth, much larger than my thumbs, ready to tear into my body. Again, the saliva dripped from that mouth, hungry for a snack. And by the size of him, a snack was all I would be.

He put two large hands on my shoulders and raised me clean up off my feet, *major*.

I knew I was a goner. Alls I could think of now was Butch, Samantha and Dooley. I would soon join them on the insides of monsters, doomed to sing songs and Happy Birthday to a zillion kids who had no idea of how or why they were there.

As Gunther chomped and slobbered all over me, I thought of the next batch of kids Cravetts would find for his monsters.

Cravetts said something before I could no longer hear him. "Well! That's four down and a few hundred to go before I rid this town of all the screaming, snot-nosed kids." Then he laughed, and I heard no more.

I guess, since I'm telling you, it's too late for you, too. There are rules for a reason. We all found out too late. Now all we can do now is sing songs on stage and talk to each other with our minds. We can't play or go to school . . . or even go to the bathroom. We are inside the monsters, doomed to live here forever. But, we do get hungry.

Don't worry. It will be feeding time again soon.

-end-

More About "Gunther's Grubbys" & Jax Jaffer

Don't take it upon yourself to right a wrong. Go to a trusted adult for help. Don't agree to do something you know is wrong just to be accepted by the group, or to "fit in." And . . . don't do dumb things like sneak out of the house at night. It's dangerous. You will get caught by someone . . . or something.

Aside from writing, Jax Laffer loves to tend to the Wild Horses of Nevada. She lives in the hills with her husband, Ed, and her granddaughter Ashley. She's a professional artist, loves movies and video games. Currently, she is working on The Blood Within, a vampire story for Yard Dog Press, and Masters of Magic, a Wizard's series.

Her first novel, *Another Side of Evil*, was published by Yard Dog Press in 2000. A short story, "The Gift," appears in *Stories That Won't Make Your Parents Hurl*, by Yard Dog Press. Her second novel, a twisted vampire novel entitled *The Blood Within* was published in 2002 by Yard Dog Press.

The Pack

by Rhonda Eudaly

The grass rustled ever so slightly. Toby watched and waited for the perfect moment to strike. He was just about to spring...

"Toby! Come home this instant!" his mother barked.

Young Toby and the rabbit both jumped at the unexpected sound. The rabbit fled to the safety of the forest while Toby turned back toward home.

"I almost had it," he muttered to himself. "My first rabbit, and I almost had it." He picked up speed so he wouldn't get into any more trouble than he was already in. He could see his mother tapping an impatient paw as she waited on the porch. All his siblings were there, watching to see what she would do to him. That's when one oversized paw caught the edge of a floppy ear, sending him tumbling nose over tail to land in a heap at his mother's feet.

"Toby," his mother sighed. "What am I going to do with you?"

Toby untangled his legs and ears, flushing with the snickers of his siblings. "I almost got a rabbit today, Mom!"

"How many times do I have to tell you to leave the rabbits alone!" his mother scolded. "They're dirty, dangerous creatures. You could get hurt."

"Yeah," one of his larger brothers taunted. "You could get hurt by the 'ittle, bitty, bunny."

"Otto, don't tease your brother."

"Yes, Mother," Otto replied with no sense of remorse, shoving Toby with his shoulder.

Toby saw it coming, but couldn't do anything to stop it. Otto was easily twice the small hound dog's size. Toby was the runt of his litter. Though everyone thought he'd someday grow into his paws and ears, not too many actually believed the small, spindly body would ever catch up. Toby's siblings reminded him of it every chance they got.

"You don't need that piece," one would say, stealing part of his dinner. "We're growing dogs. We need it more than you."

One night, Toby watched the sun go down and the stars

come out. When the first star shimmered in the deep indigo sky, Toby made a wish, just like he'd heard you did on the first star. He wished with all his young puppy might to be like the other dogs. He wanted to be big, strong, and coordinated like the rest.

As the darkness deepened, a sound came out of the woods. A haunting, howling sound that seemed to stir something deep inside Toby's young soul. He wanted to know what it was.

"Toby," his mother said, coming along side him. "Come inside, it's bed time."

Toby followed his mother toward the house when the sound came again. He stopped, sniffing the wind, trying to identify the sound. "What is that, Mother?"

Toby's mother froze a beat, then urged the pup inside. "Nothing for you to worry about, Toby. Just forget all about it."

But Toby couldn't forget about it; the sound permeated his dreams. The howls from the forest made him restless. He found himself edging more and more closely to the edge of the forest, until his mother caught him. She swatted the tender spot on his nose and sent him home. Toby yelped and cringed, he'd never seen his mother quite so angry.

"You are *never, ever* to go into the forest!" she scolded. "Never alone, never at night, and never into the forest."

"Why?" Toby asked in a pleading tone.

"The forest isn't safe for dogs," his mother replied. "And because I said so. I know what's best."

Though thoroughly chastened, Toby still felt the pull of the calls in the forest. As the days went by, the call grew louder, more insistent, and seemingly for Toby alone. None of the others seemed to hear the sound as he did. Nor did he mention it knowing the other pups would only tease him for his large ears.

Not long after that day, Toby found another opportunity to chase rabbits in the meadow. When the rabbit bolted, it went straight for the tree line. Before he knew it, Toby was well in the shadows. When he turned to go back, another dog stepped into his path. A girl dog about his own age.

"Who're you?" Toby growled, instinctively raising his hackles. "What do you want?"

"Relax, Toby, I'm a friend."

"How do you know my name?"

"Friends know each other's names."

"I don't know yours."

The girl thought a moment. "Oh, right. I'm Nyla. Wanna play?"

"I'm not allowed to play in the forest. My mother says

it's not safe."

Nyla butted her head under his chin. "Come on, it'll be okay. My mother let's me play here, and theirs."

Toby looked around and found himself surrounded by other pups, all about their same age. He wasn't sure if he should be frightened or happy. He never really had friends before. He didn't know what they were like. He was nervous. There was something wild about these pups. "I...I don't know."

"Come on, Toby," Nyla cooed. "We're going to have fun. You want to have fun, don't you?"

It was a good argument, and Toby found himself wanting to go with them. Just as he was about to turn deeper into the forest, he heard his mother calling all the pups home. His resolve broke.

"I've got to go home," he said, quickly easing past Nyla. "Maybe tomorrow."

"We'll wait for you here, Toby," Nyla told him. "You belong with us, Toby, remember that. We're your friends."

Toby couldn't think of anything else for the rest of the day. Each time Otto or one of the other pups teased him, the desire to be among dogs who actually liked him and wanted him around grew. He found himself watching the forest more and more. His mother saw it and instructed her other pups to be kinder to their smaller brother and to keep Toby away from the forest.

Otto, however, took the instructions to mean free reign to harass and torture his smaller brother. Just before bed time, Toby sat on the porch staring at the trees. The larger dog flew at him and sent them both tumbling.

"What's so special out there?" Otto demanded. "It's just a bunch of silly trees and such."

"You wouldn't understand," Toby mumbled. "Leave me alone."

Otto cuffed him. "You saying I'm stupid?"

In an uncharacteristic burst of strength and backbone, Toby shoved his brother off him. "Leave me alone. I said you wouldn't understand!"

"Then make me, runt," Otto snarled. He swatted Toby once more and sent the young pup tumbling off the porch. Toby shook himself and ran toward the forest. "That's right, runt, run away! Good riddance and don't come back!"

Toby ran into the woods. At first he didn't realize how dark and scary it was after dark. He ran, helter skelter, through the trees until he tripped over a root and went sprawling. When he got to his feet and shook himself off once more, he began to realize where he was and what he'd done. He was also very aware that he was alone.

The pup listened for the howl that had drawn him to the forest to begin with, but what was so loud at home was lost in other more frightening sounds of the forest. The shadows seemed to take on a life of their own. Toby started to shiver. It was colder in the forest at night than Toby expected, and a whole lot bigger.

"Hello?" he called out in a wavering voice. "Anyone there?"

"We're here, Toby," Nyla said, coming out of the shadows, followed by the other pups. They looked no less feral in moonlight than they had earlier. "We knew you'd come. You belong with us, you know."

"Are you sure?" Toby asked. "How can you be sure?"

"Because of the howling, Toby," Nyla told him. "We've all heard the howling, just like you. They told us your name, just like the rest of us. You're one of us now, Toby."

He wavered. He was too far into the woods to hear his mother's urgent calls, and now that he was listening, he could hear the howl once more. It was more powerful, more seductive, and insistent. It felt good to be wanted.

"Come with us, Toby," Nyla urged once more. "Be part of the pack."

"Pack? You guys are a pack?" Toby asked in surprised awe. He'd heard adults talk about packs in whispers and warning tones. They never sounded like good things then, but this didn't seem so bad.

"Does that scare you?"

Toby drew himself up proudly, full of bravado. "I'm not scared of anything."

The other dogs in the pack snickered, but Nyla hushed them with a look. "That's great, Toby. Then join us. We'll give you everything you need."

"What about my family?"

"We're your family now, Toby. Do you think that big oaf of a brother wants you back?"

Toby's lip curled in distaste. "Okay, I'm with you."

All the dogs of the pack surrounded Toby in a wild display of welcome. The newest member was hustled deeper into the forest. For the first time in as long as he could remember, Toby actually felt like he belonged somewhere. He never wanted the feeling to end.

After a few days, though, Toby began to miss his home. His new friends were great and all, but he rather missed his warm bed and regular meals. The pack ate on an irregular schedule on whatever they could find. Sometimes he didn't really want to think about where the food came from. The only good thing about it was that he was finally allowed to eat his entire meal. Nyla made sure no one took what was his. No one in the pack said no to Nyla.

"Toby, I need you to do something for me," she told him one day as they wandered the edge of the forest.

"Huh? What? Like a favor?"

"More like an initiation."

"A what?" Toby wasn't familiar with the word.

"Something you do to prove you're really one of us," she explained. "We all had to do it to be part of the pack."

"I...I...thought the howling..."

"Just marks you as one of us, we still need to know you're truly one of us."

"What do you want me to do?"

They came out of the woods in the meadow near Toby's house. The pup recognized it immediately. "This is where I used to live, why are we here?"

"Do you want to go back?"

"No..." but there was a note of uncertainty in his voice.

"Good, now prove it."

Two others of the pack came toward them, herding another pup, Otto. Nyla and the two others melted back into the circle formed by the rest of the pack, leaving Toby in the center.

"This is it, Toby. This one has hurt one of us. He tormented you, teased you, made you come to us. Now it's your turn. If you want to truly be one of us, take him."

"Take him?"

"Out. Take him out, Toby. Make him meat."

"Toby! No!" Otto cried. "You can't!"

Toby growled and bared his teeth at his brother. "Give me one good reason why not."

"I'm your brother."

"In the last few days, the pack has been more like brothers than you ever were!"

"Toby, I'm sorry!" Otto whimpered, cowering before the smaller pup. "Please don't do this."

"Come on, Toby," Nyla encouraged. "Do it. The pack stands together or not at all. You don't need him, you need us. Take your revenge on him for all he did to you. You'll be one of us forever. Do it!"

The rest of the pack began chanting softly and letting it build in strength, volume and intensity. Toby felt the chant build in his blood and bones, merging with the howling. His upper lip twitched over one of his fangs, and his eyes gleamed with a wild fire. Otto cowered before him, whimpering, and Toby reveled in it.

Suddenly, almost as quickly as it came, the spell was broken. The howling died as Toby shook his head. He saw his brother for the broken bully he really was and knew he couldn't hurt the bigger dog.

"I...I can't."

"You have to if you want to be one of us," Nyla insisted. "And you do want to be one of us don't you, Toby."

Toby looked at her. He saw her for the first time, too, with her matted coat and crusted paws. Her ribs stuck out under her fur. "Not as much as I thought. I just want to go home."

"You'll regret it, Toby. You belong with us. You're one of us."

"Yeah, maybe," Toby replied, then he indicated Otto. "But I was one of him long before I was one of you."

Nyla turned her back on Toby and headed for the trees, the pack following her. "Don't try to come back to us, Toby. You had your chance, and you blew it." She and the pack faded into the forest.

Toby's mother was overjoyed to have her son home. She found Toby on the porch just before bed time. "Thinking about the pack?"

Toby nodded. "I can still hear it, but not as strong as before."

"Probably calling someone else," his mother replied. "I feel sorry for that pup, but I'm glad to have you back. You belong here, with your family. I hope you don't forget that, or that your mother may actually know what's best."

"Aw, Mom."

"Don't 'aw, Mom' me, young man. Now go on to bed. It's late, and next time, be more careful what you wish for."

"Yes, ma'am." Toby headed inside and paused at the door. "Thanks, Mom. Now I know there's no place like home."

"Don't forget it, either. Home is the one place you'll always belong." She shooed her small son inside with a kiss on the nose, content she needn't worry about Toby forgetting that lesson any time soon.

-end-

All About "The Pack" & Rhonda Eudaly

"The Pack" has several morals, the least of which being: be careful what you wish for, you just might get it. The major moral is to beware of any group that tries to fundamentally change or control who you are - like cults and gangs, or even plain peer pressure. These can suck you in, turn you into someone you're not, and can be lethal. The last moral is to listen to mothers - they're not as bad as most kids think - and they're usually right. I've come a long way on the better judgment, advice and support, and greater experience of my parents.

Rhonda Eudaly lives in Fort Worth, Texas, where she is a self-proclaimed "Jane-of-All-Trades." She's worked in offices, in banking, in radio, helped build radio stations, been an audio technician, and even dug the occasional ditch to support her writing habit. Currently, Rhonda's supporting that habit and her cat, Dixon, by substitute teaching high school. She likes to swing dance; to spend time with friends and family; to collect smiley faces, all things alien, and reindeer at Christmas. Her two passions are writing and music, and she remains a hopeless romantic.

Rhonda Eudaly has been published previously in Dallas regional press, and *Christian Family Magazine*, but this is her first professional anthology. She can also be found in *Beyond the Skyline*, a tribute to the victims of September 11.

Puppy Love
by Garrett Peck

"*B*ark! Bark!"

"Shh!" nine-year-old Aaron MacKenzie told the scruffy little puppy he held in his arms. "If mommy hears you, she'll make you go away."

The puppy responded by licking his face. The slobbery tongue tickled his cheek and made him giggle. Aaron hugged it tight against his chest.

He had found it sitting in a box by the side of the road as he walked home from school. Somebody's dog must have had babies and the owner couldn't find a home for it. It was a skinny little thing, covered in matted brown hair. It wasn't the cutest he'd ever seen, but that didn't matter. He'd played with it for a while. When it came time to go home he'd tried to say goodbye to it, but it insisted on following him. It *wanted* to be his dog. He could tell. So he had hid it under his jacket and sneaked it up to his room.

For as long as Aaron could remember, all he had ever wanted was a dog of his own. Every year he'd ask his mother to let him have one for his birthday or Christmas, but she always said no. He promised he'd take care of it: feed it, take it for walks and clean up after it if it peed or pooped in the house, but his mother adamantly refused. She said money was too tight. She couldn't afford to feed it or take it to the vets for shots. She said there was no one to look after it while she was at work and he was at school. She said she didn't want hair all over her furniture and fleas in her carpet. She said a dog had bitten her when she was a little girl and she didn't want that to happen to him. Mom always had plenty of excuses, but he didn't believe any of them. She didn't want him to have a dog because she was *mean*. She claimed she loved him, but how could he believe that when she wouldn't let him have the one thing he wanted above all else?

As Aaron thought about how angry this made him, he squeezed the puppy harder than he meant to. It yelped.

"No, puppy! You've got to be quiet!" he admonished it.

"Aaron?" came his mother's voice. "What was that?"

"Nothing!" he shouted back.

"That didn't sound like nothing to me. Are you hurt?"

He could hear her footsteps heading toward his room. Knowing she'd take the puppy away from him if she saw it, he quickly deposited it in his bedroom closet. It stuck its head out as he tried to shut the closet door. Its nose got squashed between the folding doors. It squealed again and drew back.

The pace of his mother's footsteps picked up, so he hurried to his bedroom door to head her off. He was a moment too late. In her concern, she flung his door open forcefully. The edge struck him in the forehead. He cried out as he fell back on his butt, clasping a hand to his head. He felt liquid trickle through his fingers and knew he must be bleeding.

"Oh, baby!" his mother cried out in alarm. "I'm so sorry! Let me see."

She pulled his hand away from his forehead and examined the wound. She drew in a sharp breath as she saw the blood running down his face, mixing with his tears. "Oh, honey! Stay here. Let me get a towel to hold against it."

Aaron held his hand against the wound and sobbed as his mother ran off and returned with the promised towel. She gently moved his hand aside and wiped up the blood surrounding the wound. She couldn't keep it clear for long. As soon as she wiped off the cut, blood would instantly begin to drool from it again.

"This looks bad," she surmised. "We better go to the doctor. It might need stitches."

"No, mommy!" Aaron wailed. "I don't want stitches!"

"I know, Aaron. But that cut looks too deep. You don't want to have an ugly scar on your face, do you?"

Sniff. "No."

"Okay, then. Let's go."

Taking Aaron by the upper arm, she pulled him to his feet. She kept her hand clamped to his arm as she pulled him toward the bedroom door. That's when the puppy whimpered from inside his closet and scratched its claws against the door. She stopped and looked back at the closet, her grip tightening.

"What was that, Aaron?"

"N...nothing, Mommy."

"I don't think so."

She released his arm, walked over to the closet and pulled the door open. The puppy emerged, wagging its tail. It went straight to her ankles and started licking. She yanked her foot back with an "Ugh!" She turned to her injured son.

"What is this?"

"A... a puppy."

"So this is what you were trying to hide. Haven't we discussed this before? Go get in the car. I'll take care of this mangy mutt."

She reached down to seize the puppy. The quick movement startled it and it squirted pee on the rug. "Ugh!" she cried again, holding it away from her. "You see what dogs do?"

"I'll clean it up, mommy," Aaron offered meekly.

"You'll do no such thing. We need to get you to the doctor. Go get in the car."

Still sobbing, now more about the loss of the puppy than the pain of his wound, Aaron obeyed his mother. She followed behind him. As soon as she shut the front door behind them, she put the puppy down and told it to scat.

"Please don't leave him out here, mom!" he begged. "He could get run over!"

"What else can I do with him? I can't leave him in the house. You shouldn't have brought him here in the first place."

"But he followed me home! He wants to be my puppy."

"We'll discuss this in the car, honey. You're bleeding badly and I need to get you to the doctor. Let's go."

She grabbed him tightly around the arm and guided him towards their old Toyota. Sulking, Aaron got in the passenger side while his mother sat in the driver's seat. She fastened her seat belt and double-checked his to be sure it was secure.

Once they were on the road, Aaron asked, "Why can't I keep the puppy, mommy?"

"Oh, Aaron. We've gone through this so many times before. You know we can't keep a dog. Besides, he probably belongs to someone else."

"No, he doesn't! Someone left him in a box on the side of the road. He doesn't have a home. Can't I keep him? Please?"

"No, honey. I'm sorry. Our lease says we can't have pets."

"But they won't know! I'll keep him up in my room. No one will know he's there."

"You can't just keep him locked up in your bedroom. You'd have to take him out for walks. The whole neighborhood would know you had him."

"I don't care! I want him!"

"I know, sweetie. I wish we lived someplace where you could have one, but we don't."

"Then why don't we move?"

"You know we can't afford to do that. Ever since your father disappeared I've barely been making ends meet as it is. I don't even know how I'm going to pay your doctor's bill."

Aaron stamped his feet. *"You're mean! I'll bet you hurt me on purpose!"*

"Honey, that's ridiculous," she said, her voice softening. "You know I love you more than anything in the whole wide world. I'd never do anything to hurt you. It was just an accident... and it never would have happened if you hadn't brought that dirty dog in the house. But don't you worry; Dr. Nicholson will fix you right up."

Dr. Nicholson examined Aaron's wound as Mrs. MacKenzie hovered over them, wringing her hands. "Yesiree," he said in his folksy voice, "that's a nasty one. I think a few stitches are in order."

"Will it hurt?" Aaron asked.

"Just a little, but not too much," Dr. Nicholson said. "I'm going to give you a shot of Novocaine. That will hurt a tiny bit, but it will numb the wound so you won't feel any pain when I give you the stitches. Okay?"

Sniff. "I guess."

Dr. Nicholson smiled and ruffled the hair on the back of Aaron's neck. "You're a brave boy."

At first Aaron thought Dr. Nicholson had lied to him. The little needle of the Novocaine shot hurt more than a tiny bit, but then the numbness set in. He could feel the needle poking through his skin as the doctor stitched him up, but it didn't really hurt like he thought it would.

"There, that wasn't too bad, was it?" Dr. Nicholson said with a smile after he finished. "Now all it needs is a bandage. Mrs. MacKenzie, would you do me a favor?"

"Certainly, doctor."

"Go to the desk and ask Cathy to write a prescription for Augmentin and bring it to me. He's not allergic to Penicillin, is he?"

"No, he's had it before," Mrs. MacKenzie confirmed. "There were no problems."

"Good. Thank you."

After she left, Dr. Nicholson looked at Aaron. He smiled as he applied the bandage, but something about his expression seemed strained.

"How did you get this cut, Aaron?"

"My mom did it."

The doctor's brow furrowed in concern. "She did? Why?"

"She was mad at me. This cute little puppy followed me home and I took it up to my room. My mom *hates* dogs."

"She does? That doesn't sound very nice. I love them, myself. I've got three at home."

"Really? Gee, I wish I could see them."

"I wish you could, too. Now how about those bruises around your arm? How did you get those?"

Aaron looked down at his arm and saw the ring of bruises the doctor was talking about. He hadn't noticed them earlier, but they were right where his mother had gripped him as she pulled him toward the car.

"Mom did that, too."

"Really? Does your mom hurt you like this very often?"

At first Aaron was going to answer honestly, but then he thought about it. Maybe if he told Dr. Nicholson that his mom *did* hurt him all the time she would get in trouble. That would teach her to not let him have a dog.

"Yes! She gets mad and hits me all the time."

"You mean she spanks you? Or does she do other things?"

"Sometimes. Sometimes she smacks my face. Sometimes she kicks me, too." None of it was true, but Aaron thought it sounded pretty good.

"Mothers aren't supposed to do that to their children. You know that, don't you?"

"Yeah, I guess so. But she's my mom. What can I do about it?" Aaron started to sob, figuring that would make Dr. Nicholson feel sorrier for him. He could tell it was working when the doctor put a gentle hand on his shoulder and rubbed.

"I can help you, Aaron. What your mother's done to you is wrong. Being your mother doesn't give her the right to hurt you like this. Now I'm going to ask you a serious question and I want you to think about it very carefully before you answer. Are you afraid to go home with your mother?"

Aaron pretended to think hard, but inside he was rejoicing. Maybe if he said he was scared to go home with his mother he could go to Dr. Nicholson's house instead. Then he could have *three* dogs!

"I don't want to go home with mommy. I got blood on her favorite towel and she's going to hit me again." He cried some more to make it look convincing.

Dr. Nicholson pulled Aaron into his arms and held him. "It's okay, Aaron. Don't worry. You don't have to go home with your mother if you don't want to."

The door to the examination room opened and Nurse Cathy came in with a prescription pad in hand. "What's the matter?" she asked.

Without loosening his hug on Aaron, the doctor said, "Get HRS on the phone, Cathy. It appears Mrs. MacKenzie has been abusing her son."

Aaron, his face buried in the doctor's chest, grinned. His mom would be in big trouble now! She should have let him keep his puppy.

Aaron was able to hear a little bit of the conversation between his mother and Dr. Nicholson in the office lobby, especially when she raised her voice. "What?" he heard her say. "That's absurd! It was an accident. I'd never hurt Aaron on purpose. I love him! He's all I live for!" He expected her to come bursting into the room to drag him out, but she didn't. Instead, Dr. Nicholson appeared a few minutes later, along with a woman he'd never seen before.

"Aaron, this is Mrs. Griffin. She's going to take you to a place where you'll be safe until we're sure your mother isn't going to hurt you anymore."

Aaron was crestfallen. He had thought he'd get to go home with Dr. Nicholson. "Can't I just go to your house? I want to meet your dogs."

Dr. Nicholson looked at Mrs. Griffin. "Aaron loves dogs," he told her. "His mother won't let him have one. That's why she hurt him today. He brought an abandoned puppy that followed him home into the house. She seems to be phobic about canines because a dog bit her when she was a little girl."

Mrs. Griffin nodded her head sagely. "I suspect it was because she was abusing it somehow. Her type often begins by tormenting animals when they're young, then they graduate to abusing their offspring when they become mothers." She turned to face Aaron. "I'm sorry, but you can't go to Dr. Nicholson's. I have to take you to a state approved foster home for a few days until we can make sure it's safe for you to go home again. And since I know you like animals so much, I know just the family for you. They run a dog kennel. Why, they must have thirty or forty dogs at least!"

Aaron perked up. "Really? They have that many?"
"They sure do."

That didn't seem too fair to Aaron. If these people could have that many dogs, why couldn't he have just one? But that didn't matter. He was going to live in a house with more dogs than he'd ever dreamed of having. He was glad he had lied to Dr. Nicholson. This was working out even better than he thought.

Mrs. Griffin explained what was happening to Aaron's mother on the ride over to the foster home. She was going to stay at the hospital for a few days so psychiatrists could examine her and make sure she understood that she couldn't hit him ever again. Aaron felt a little guilty about that, but it didn't sound too bad. It sounded like when she'd send him up to his room for doing something bad. That was okay with Aaron. He thought she deserved to be punished for not letting him have a dog.

But he was much less interested in his mother than in learning about the Castellanos, the family he would be staying with. They ran a kennel on their property. They kept dogs for people who went out of town on vacation, but also had a lot of their own. They even bred Rottweilers to sell to other people. Aaron could hardly imagine having so many dogs. He just knew he was going to love it there. Mrs. Griffin told him that as well as taking care of dogs and other animals, they also took care of children that needed a place to stay.

"They're such wonderful people," Mrs. Griffin enthused. "So full of love for all living things."

The car pulled up to a gate. Mrs. Griffin honked her horn. Aaron saw a sign posted on the gate featuring the silhouette of a Rottweiler and the words, "I CAN MAKE IT TO THE GATE IN 3.5 SECONDS. CAN YOU?" Peering into the yard through the gate, Aaron saw more dogs than he'd ever seen gathered in one place. Many of them were big, black Rottweilers, but he also spied a Collie, a Poodle, a Great Dane and a couple of Golden Retrievers, as well as several other unclassifiable mutts. It was dog heaven. He also spied several cats stalking around the yard. Cats were okay, he guessed, but it was the dogs that really excited him. They rushed up to the gate, barking and wagging their tails. They were excited to see him, too!

There was a long white building several feet behind the fence. It had a door facing the road, which opened up and revealed a tall man with shoulder-length, salt-and-pepper hair and a long, thick beard. A much shorter woman in an orange sundress, who appeared to be a few years younger than the man, followed him. They broke into friendly grins and waved. Aaron could hear more dogs barking inside the building. Mrs. Castellano shut the kennel's door, then followed her husband to the gate. She shooed away the dogs as her husband unlocked the gate and swung it open, allowing Mrs. Griffin's car to pull in. Mr. Castellano shut the gate behind them, but didn't bother locking it.

Mrs. Griffin and Aaron got out of the car. Several of the dogs loose in the yard immediately came up to them and started sniffing.

"Hello there, young man," Mr. Castellano said. "I hope you're not afraid of dogs."

"No, sir!" Aaron said. "I love dogs!" He began petting the closest one—the collie—who responded by licking his hand enthusiastically. The other dogs moved in closer, demanding their share of attention. Aaron was more than happy to give it to them.

Mrs. Castellano laughed. "It looks like they love you, too!"

Mrs. Griffin joined in the laughter. "They sure do! That's why I brought this boy to you. His mother had beaten him for bringing home a stray pup. He needed eight stitches."

Mrs. Castellano gasped. "How horrible!"

"I'll say," her husband agreed. "All good boys should have a dog of their own. Why, boys and dogs go together like bread and butter!"

"Aaron," Mrs. Griffin called, "come over here and meet the Castellanos."

Aaron didn't really want to give up petting the dogs, but he obeyed. He needn't have worried. The dogs followed and stood right by him as he shook the Castellanos' hands.

Mrs. Griffin explained that she would be going by his house tomorrow and picking up some of his clothes to bring over. She promised to be by in the early afternoon. Were there any toys he wanted her to bring? He told her not to worry about those. Who needed toys when he had all these real live dogs to play with? And that's exactly what he did as the adults had one of their boring grown up talks. He ran laughing, the dogs bounding happily behind him.

After Mrs. Griffin left—reminding Aaron she'd be back tomorrow with his clothes—Mr. Castellano had asked him if he wanted to help feed the dogs in the kennel while his wife fixed their dinner. Aaron readily agreed.

For all the dogs that were allowed to roam the yard, there were even more inside the kennel. Aaron asked Mr. Castellano why some of the dogs had to stay in the kennel and others didn't. He explained that a lot of these dogs belonged to other people and they were just taking care of them until their owners came home. They wanted to make sure these dogs didn't get hurt fighting with the others. Some of the Rottweilers, he explained, had to stay in cages because they were too aggressive. Mr. Castellano fed these dogs himself, but allowed Aaron to feed all the others. He especially enjoyed feeding Sheena, the mama Rottweiler. She had a litter of five puppies. They were the cutest things Aaron had ever seen — just tiny balls of fluff.

"Can I have one of the puppies when I go home?" Aaron asked.

"I'd be happy to give you one, but that would be up to your mother. I thought she didn't like dogs."

"She doesn't, but I think she may let me have one now." *And if she doesn't*, he thought to himself, *I'll just tell Dr. Nicholson she hit me again. He'll put her back in the hospital until she'll let me have one.*

"Joe! Aaron!" Mrs. Castellano yelled from the front porch. "Dinner's ready!"

"Sounds like it's our turn to eat," Mr. Castellano said. "You hungry?"

"Yes, sir!" Aaron said, matching Mr. Castellano's smile. The man put an arm around his shoulder as he led Aaron to the family's house.

The dining room table was laid out with bowls and big soupspoons. As soon as Aaron and Mr. Castellano were seated, Mrs. Castellano ladled out huge servings of a deliciously fragrant beef stew into their bowls. Aaron picked up his spoon and prepared to dig in, but Mr. Castellano put a restraining hand on his arm before he could raise the spoon to his mouth.

"Not yet, Aaron," Mr. Castellano said. "We have to say grace first."

Grace wasn't something Aaron had to say back home, except on Thanksgiving, but he knew how to do it. He clasped his hands together, closed his eyes and lowered his head. Mr. Castellano recited a prayer unlike any he'd heard before.

"Oh, Great Old Ones, who existed before the beginning of time, bless this food upon our table. May it provide us sustenance so we may continue to serve your earthly incarnation until the time is ripe for you to reclaim your rightful dominion. We, your humble servants, beseech this in your names — Nyarlathotep, Stalker Among the Stars; Azathoth, He in the Gulf; Shub-Niggurath, Goat with a Thousand Young; and Great

Cthulhu, He Who Lies Dreaming. Amen!"

Although Aaron didn't understand much of the prayer with all the funny names Mr. Castellano intoned, he joined Mrs. Castellano in saying "amen" as a show of respect. He didn't want to upset them, because there was always a chance his mother would remain obstinate in her refusal to allow a dog in the house. If that turned out to be the case, he would rather stay here.

The beef stew was tastier than any his mother had ever prepared. She just heated up tins of Dinty Moore. His mom always claimed she was too tired from working all day to cook real meals, usually settled for heating up TV dinners or something from a can. Mrs. Castellano had obviously made hers from scratch.

As he brought another spoonful to his mouth, a loud screeching sound caught him off-guard and made him drop his spoon. He looked to the Castellanos for an explanation. The couple were staring at the cellar door with concerned expressions.

"It sounds hungry," Mrs. Castellano said.

"But I just fed it three days ago," her husband replied. "Usually it only demands food once a week."

"It's getting much bigger, though. It must need more."

Another horrific shriek emanated from the basement. It didn't sound like any animal Aaron was familiar with. He couldn't help being curious. "What's hungry?" he asked.

"Never you mind," Mrs. Castellano said. "I think you better bring it a snack, Joe." A third unidentifiable cry from beneath the floorboards seemed to agree with her. "One of Sheena's brood, I think."

Mr. Castellano nodded, wiped his lips with a napkin and stood. He strode resignedly toward the front door.

"Where's he going?" Aaron asked.

"He's doing what must be done. Don't you worry about it," Mrs. Castellano declared.

"But..."

"No questions. Eat your stew like a good boy."

Aaron did as commanded, but the stew didn't taste as good as it had a few moments ago. Even so, he had nearly cleaned the bowl when Mr. Castellano returned. He held one of the Rottweiler pups in his arms. He showed it to his wife.

"I chose a nice fat one. Think this will hold it for a while?"

"He should do fine," his wife agreed.

A ravenous subterranean growl concurred. Mr. Castellano carried the pup through the basement door, which he closed behind him. Even over the hungry rumblings of whatever was down there, Aaron could hear the puppy whining in fear.

"Why is he taking that puppy downstairs?" Aaron demanded.

"Everything that lives must eat," Mrs. Castellano said. "It may seem cruel, but that is nature's way."

"You mean he's going to feed the puppy to something down there?"

Mrs. Castellano's silence answered for her.

Aaron couldn't allow this to happen. He sprang from his seat, raced to the basement door and flung it open.

"No! You mustn't go down there!" Mrs. Castellano warned, but Aaron didn't listen. He hurried down the steps and caught up with the tall man holding the whimpering puppy in two out-thrust hands, preparing to toss it down.

"Stop!" Aaron yelled. "You can't do that!"

Mr. Castellano turned around, still holding the puppy. "Go back upstairs, Aaron. You don't understand. The shoggoth must be fed. If not..."

Aaron didn't wait for the explanation. He snatched at the puppy, saying, "Give it!" Mr. Castellano fought back, trying to pull the puppy from his grasp. Being only nine years old, Aaron didn't have enough strength to fight the man. Still, he clung tenaciously to the squirming young dog. Mr. Castellano lifted it away from him, but he hung on with all his might. His feet raised off the staircase, but his fingers slipped away from the puppy's sleek fur.

Aaron landed on the uneven steps and lost his balance. He tumbled down the remaining few stairs. Something soft and squishy broke his fall. Before he could even guess what he had landed on, a slimy tentacle wrapped itself around his middle and started to haul him away. He tilted his head back, trying to see what had a hold of him.

What he saw made him scream louder than he knew he was capable of.

He was being pulled toward an open, beaked mouth that dripped gooey green saliva. He struggled as best he could, but his flailing limbs could find no purchase on the viscous surface of the squid-like monstrosity. He was drawn inexorably closer to its greedy, gaping jaws.

"Mommy!" Aaron shouted. "Help me, Mommy! I'm sorry I lied to the doctor! Mommy, please!"

But it was far too late for that. She was no longer there to protect him. He had seen to that himself.

The last thing he heard before the fishy smelling mouth closed over him was the excited barking of the puppy that would never be his.

-end-

About "Puppy Love" & Garrett Peck

"Puppy Love" is a story about mistaken intentions. If Aaron had listened to his mother, he would have understood that she wasn't refusing to allow him to have a puppy because she wanted to, but because they were not allowed to have one. He mistakes her denial for lack of love, then betrays her by lying to his doctor. He thinks this terrible lie will get him what he wants, but learns too late that all he's done is separate himself from the one person who loved him above all else.

The lesson here is that lies will never get you what you want; they will come back to haunt you and get you in big trouble. This tale was inspired by a story a friend of mine told me about some friends of his family. They had a very rude little girl who never obeyed them. They tried talking to her, but she refused to listen. When all else failed, they finally gave her the spanking she deserved. Instead of accepting her punishment, she called HRS on them. Those government folks came in and told the parents they weren't allowed to spank their girl for being bad. How else were they supposed to teach her right from wrong if she wouldn't listen to them? It would serve her right if the state did take her away from her home. Then she might have realized how good she has it. The Castellano family is based on a real family I know who run a dog kennel. They are very loving people who have adopted four children and raised them as their own. They have lots of animals, but fortunately no shoggoths!

The author lives in the nation's oldest city, St. Augustine, Florida, where he has acted in, produced and directed many plays. He was once a tour guide for A Ghostly Experience, where he led people around by lantern light and told them true ghost stories about St. Augustine. He's even seen a ghost himself and liked telling that story best.

You can find more of Garrett's stories in the Yard Dog Press books *Stories That Won't Make Your Parents Hurl*, *Bubbas of the Apocalypse*, and *Beyond the Skyline*, as well as *Brainbox: The Real Horror* (Irrational Press) and the Lone Wolf Publications anthologies *Stones* and *The Red, Red Robin Project*. Also for Lone Wolf Publications, he co-edited the anthologies *Personal Demons* (with Brian A. Hopkins) and two volumes of creature stories called *Tooth and Claw* (with J. F. Gonzalez). He reviews books for publications like *Gauntlet,* and *Cemetery Dance*, and served as chairman of the 2001 Bram Stoker Award Additions Jury for the Horror Writers Association. He currently runs the *Hellnotes* newsletter.

The Wigglers

by Bennie Grezlik

Marty grabbed her lunchbox and headed for the door. As always, her brother pushed his way ahead of her.

When they were on the sidewalk waiting for the bus, she said to him, "Open your mouth."

"Huh?"

"Yeah, that was enough." She made a face. "Jeez, Toby, your teeth look like you ate diaper gravy for breakfast. Try brushing them like once a month or so."

"Shows how much you know, 'Martha Stewart.' I brush my teeth all the time. I can't help it they look dirty. It's my genes, or something. Blame Mom and Dad."

"Is that what you tell Mom? That you have yellow teeth because of genes? Ha! If she buys that, I'm sneaking out to the mall tonight and I'll tell her I had an out-of-body experience."

"As a matter of fact, I did tell her something like that. She sort of believes me, but she wants to send me to a dentist."

They watched the bus come round the corner two blocks down. Marty peeled a stick of gum and popped it into her mouth. "Well, I don't buy it. I know you better than Mom. You hate brushing your teeth. Want a stick?"

"Sure."

"Just don't chew with your mouth open, okay? Honestly, Toby, I don't care what you do. But you might start thinking about, you know, what the girls think."

Toby pursed his lips and made a rude sound. "You can wake up now, Marty. I couldn't care less what your friends think."

"Oh? That's too bad, because Ginny kind of has a crush on you. But she asked me about your teeth."

"Get real, Lucille. That didn't happen and I wouldn't care if it did."

The bus screeched to a stop in front of them. "Suit yourself, Bro. But if you pass sixth grade, and that's a big 'if' after they held you back two years ago, you'll be the only guy going into Junior High without a girlfriend."

"You are so full of it."

They got on the bus. Toby spotted his friends at the back and started towards them. Marty grabbed him, pulled his head down to hers and whispered loudly, "Remember, dental hygiene!"

Toby elbowed her and twisted away. As casually as he could, he glanced at Ginny sitting near the front as he raced down the isle.

Marty plopped down next to Ginny.

"Omigod, you told him, didn't you?"

"I didn't tell him."

"You told him."

"Okay, maybe I told him. Let's just see what happens."

"Omigod, you told him."

That night, Toby locked himself in the bathroom. He turned on the water, wet his toothbrush, then squirted a glob of toothpaste into the drain. God, how he hated brushing his teeth. And he didn't see why he had to. They were his teeth, after all. How long had it been, now?

He'd gotten caught that time when he'd forgotten to lock the door and his Dad walked in. He was standing there with the brush in his hand and the water running, and his Dad had said to go ahead, not to mind him, he was just going to shave.

So he'd brushed his teeth. That had been months ago. Since then, he'd faked it every night. Now Marty was harassing him about it. He liked his sister, but she should mind her own business. And that stuff about Ginny? Sure, he thought Ginny was a hottie, but he didn't believe Ginny had said anything about him. Marty was just pulling his chain.

He looked in the mirror. He wasn't bad looking, in his estimation. Could Ginny have said that? Especially about his teeth?

He opened his mouth for a survey. His teeth were okay. Sure, they were a little yellow, but what of it? There were probably a lot of cultures that didn't bother with stupid rituals like brushing teeth.

Light gleamed off the side of his tongue. Or was it? He moved his tongue around to get a better view. There was something... No, it was just saliva on his tongue, he was sure. He shut his mouth and ran his tongue around the inside of his teeth. They felt rough, but he was used to that.

He turned off the water and went to bed. He didn't go to sleep right away. He kept feeling the roughness of his teeth. He wanted to go look in the mirror again, but that would be silly, he told himself.

The nice thing about being in the sixth grade at John Glenn Elementary school, was that you got to have your pick of which period to take gym class. Toby had chosen fifth period because he knew at the beginning of the year that Ginny was taking girl's gym sixth period. That meant he could finish his shower early and hit the hall as soon as the bell rang. He would have an excellent chance of "accidentally" bumping into Ginny on her way to gym.

Today was one of those times. When he saw her coming down the hall, he dropped a quarter, and then awkwardly scrambled for it under the feet of the passing students. His timing was perfect because, as he had hoped, she found the quarter for him.

"Is this what you're looking for, Toby?"

"Uh, yeah, thanks. How's it goin'."

"Okay."

"Uh, well, that's good. I guess. I got to go."

"Wait," Ginny said. "I was thinking. The Spring dance is coming up, and I know it'll be crawling with parents, but it still might be fun. Maybe if you're not taking anyone... Are you? Taking anyone, I mean?"

Toby stuck his hands in his pockets and tried to act casual. "Naw. I never even thought about it. You think it would be fun?"

Ginny shook her head.

"Do you wanna go?"

"I sure would."

He'd done it. He'd asked Ginny on a date. And she accepted! He grinned at her and she laughed. Then he felt something moving in his mouth, and it wasn't his tongue. He put his hand over his mouth.

"Toby, are you okay?"

"Yeah," he mumbled. "Gotta go. See you later."

The first bell rang, but he rushed into the boy's room anyway. Luckily, it was empty. He looked into the mirror with his mouth wide open. He jumped back and gurgled a strangled sound as he saw something move along the back of his teeth.

He didn't want to look again but he had to. He crept up to the mirror. Some kind of creature, like a worm, maybe, brown and shiny, wiggled between his back teeth and his tongue. As he watched in horror, it pulled itself into his gums and disappeared.

He waited a few seconds, then lightly ran his tongue over

his teeth. There was nothing there but that roughness he had felt the night before.

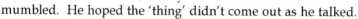

He got some toilet paper and wiped away the tears that had been running down his cheek. His hands were shaking.

The tardy bell rang as he stumbled out of the boy's room. When he tried to enter his Social Studies classroom, Mr. Blevins gave him a tardy slip to take to the Principal's office.

"But I was sick," Toby mumbled. He hoped the 'thing' didn't come out as he talked.

"Sick, huh?" said Mr. Blevins. "Then go to the Nurse's office so she can check you out."

"Can't I just call my mother to come get me?"

"You have to see the Nurse first. Those are the rules."

Toby walked to the Nurse's office with a sense of dread. What would he tell her? He decided that he couldn't tell the truth.

Mrs. Bailey, the Nurse, sat in a straight-backed chair behind a wooden desk whose top layer of varnish had been worn away from years of contact with her stern elbows. She watched him suspiciously as he came in.

"What is your problem, young man?"

"Bad headache," Toby mumbled. "Can I call my Mom to pick me up?"

"We'll see. What's your name?"

"Toby McGuire."

"First, Mr. McGuire, let's take your temperature."

Toby hadn't expected this. He watched as Mrs. Bailey peeled the paper cover from a sterilized thermometer. Would the thing in his mouth go berserk when he stuck that glass tube in there? He felt sweat roll from his forehead.

With his teeth clamped shut, he slowly slipped the thermometer between his cheek and his teeth on the side away from where he'd seen the thing.

"Put it under your tongue," Mrs. Bailey ordered, looking at him strangely. "Is your mouth okay? Can you open it normally?"

"It's okay," he mumbled. He loosened his teeth enough to get the thermometer into position.

"And don't bite it," said Mrs. Bailey.

He nodded. The seconds crept past on tiptoes. Something moved in the back of his mouth and he did almost bite the thermometer in two, in spite of what Mrs. Bailey had told him.

Mrs. Bailey finally said, "Okay, gimme."

She looked at the instrument for a moment. "Well, you do have a fever. One oh one. What's your mother's number?"

"**P**sst. Marty. Come here."

Marty threw her backpack into her room and went to Toby's door.

"What's up, Bro? Mom tells me you got a bad headache."

He pulled her in and shut the door. "Yeah, she made me take some Tylenol. That was the hard part, trying to wash down those pills."

"Why are you talking like a gangster? You got cotton in your mouth or something?"

"'Something' is right. I can't talk to anyone but you about it. No one would believe me."

"Ginny told me that you asked her to the dance, then acted all funny, like you got a sudden toothache."

Toby paced the room like an angry cat. "What would you say if I told you I had some kind of alien creature in my mouth that comes out of my gums?"

"Yeah, right. What kind of alien creature, Toby? The Tooth Fairy?"

"It's not funny, Marty! Something is in my mouth that shouldn't be there."

"Let me see."

"It's not there right now, but take a look anyway."

Marty peered into his mouth. "All I see is a few dark spots on your rear teeth. Those are cavities, Bro. You need to start taking care of your teeth."

Toby went to the mirror above his dresser. As he watched, four wigglers slowly emerged from his back lower gums. Now they were on both sides.

"Look! Look!"

Marty came over to him. Toby held his mouth wide for her, but he felt the wigglers receding.

"I don't see anything, Toby. I smell something though! Phew!" She fanned her hand in front of her face.

"They went back in! They don't want you to see them."

"Right. Toby, you need to see a Dentist. Maybe a shrink, too."

"I'm not crazy! They're really there. Besides, I told Mom that maybe my teeth had something to do with my headache. She looked at me funny, but called the dentist anyway. He had a cancellation tomorrow morning, so I have an appointment. I have to find out what's going on."

"You could also brush your teeth, man. It wouldn't kill you."

Toby looked thoughtful. "Maybe you're right. Maybe a good brushing will chase those things away." He looked in the mirror again. "They're coming out again. I'm going to keep watching in the mirror while you take a look. Maybe you can see them."

"Toby... "

"Please, Marty. Just kind of sneak up nice and easy."

She did as he asked, but the wigglers went back in as soon as she could see the back of his mouth.

Toby sat down on his the bed, tears rolling down his cheeks.

Marty sat beside him. "It's going to be all right, Bro. The dentist will find out what's going on."

Toby looked at her. "Promise you won't tell Mom."

"Maybe she should know."

"No! Then they will send me to a shrink."

"Okay, Bro." She got up and went to the door. "Try brushing your teeth, okay?"

He turned on the camcorder and propped it on his dresser so that it could see what he could see in the mirror. Maybe there wasn't enough light. He found his flashlight and shone it into his mouth. And waited. They would come out, sooner or later. He waited. After a half hour, he put the camcorder away. They quickly came out with a vengeance.

He locked the door, turned on the water, and grabbed the toothpaste tube in one hand and his brush in the other. Everything was the same as every night, but this time he really was going to brush his teeth.

He squirted a big gob of paste onto the brush. He opened his mouth and looked in the mirror. Nothing. He put the brush in his mouth and held it there a second, waiting for them to do something. Nothing. He brushed the front of his teeth with light strokes. He felt them moving. He almost hurled but he grabbed the sink and steadied himself.

He opened his mouth as he brushed and watched. There

were maybe six of them wiggling around in the back as if they were on fire. He moved the brush to his back teeth. The wigglers withdrew. He stroked his back teeth gently.

A sharp pain stabbed into his back teeth. He threw the brush into the mirror and slapped his hands over his mouth to keep from screaming. It felt as if they were squeezing the nerves of his teeth.

He quickly rinsed his mouth and looked into the mirror. They popped back out, wiggling in victory. The pain subsided. He cleaned the mirror of toothpaste, then sat down on the commode seat, his head in his hands.

"**O**pen wide."

"You're not going to poke around in there, are you? I won't let you look if you're going to poke around."

"Take it easy," Dr. Smolen said. "I just want to look. See, I'm not holding anything but a mirror."

Toby opened up, cautiously. After a minute Dr. Smolen said, "I see a couple of bad cavities."

"Nothing else?"

"No, not at the moment. The x-rays show some root deterioration, maybe a little more than normal for your age, but I think we can stop that."

"Is there, like, anything funny on the x-ray? Maybe something you've never seen before?"

Dr. Smolen laughed. "Not really. I think you're feeling a little guilty because I can see you haven't been taking care of your teeth. When's the last time you brushed?"

"Uh, I tried to brush last night."

"You tried? Brushing's not hard, Toby."

"It is for me."

Dr. Smolen sighed. "Okay, let me take a closer look."

"What's that?"

"It's just a little pick so I can move your gum back to see how far those cavities have gotten below the gum line. I promise it won't hurt."

"Please, be really, really careful."

"I promise. Come on, open up."

Toby opened his mouth. He was prepared for pain if it meant that Dr. Smolen saw the wigglers. He felt the metal pick touch a tooth in back.

"You've got a lot of tartar and plaque back here."

The pick moved to a different tooth. He thought he was prepared, but he wasn't. He screamed. Dr. Smolen jumped back.

Toby held a hand over his mouth. "Uh, uh, uh... "

"I'm sorry, Toby, I had no idea your teeth were that sensitive."

Toby wiped his mouth with a towel. "They did it. They mess with the nerves, or something. Did you see them?"

"See who?"

"You would know if you saw them. Let me borrow your little mirror."

"Uh, okay."

Toby looked. They were out, wiggling away. Even as Toby turned his mouth to Dr. Smolen and gestured for him to look, he felt them go back.

"Really Toby, I know what's in there. I already had a look, remember?"

Toby ran his hands through his hair in frustration. "Doctor, I'm going to tell you something and you're going to think I'm crazy. But just listen to me, okay?"

Toby told his story from beginning to end, and added, "They're smart. They know when I'm trying to show them to somebody. The even understand about camcorders. Please Doctor, I need someone to believe me."

Dr. Smolen placed his hand on Toby's arm and said, "Let me have another look. I promise I won't put anything in your mouth. I just need to adjust the lights. I'm going to use this magnifier so I can really see what's back there."

Reassured, Toby opened up. Dr. Smolen peered into his mouth with a hand-held magnifier for a long minute.

"Those cavities look a little unusual, so maybe you have something there."

Toby exhaled his relief. At last, someone who could help him.

"Tell you what. I need to call one of my associates to see if my theory checks out."

"What theory?"

"About your condition, of course. I've never seen this before, but maybe others have. Why don't you relax for a few minutes while I call. We're going to get to the bottom of this."

Dr. Smolen left the examining room and Toby tried to relax. Maybe this other guy, another dentist, he guessed, would know what this was all about. He leaned back into the contoured dentist's char. Then he sat straight up. They were wiggling again.

Toby got up and paced the room. The door was cracked so he pulled it open. There was activity at the reception desk down the hall. He saw a white-smocked dental assistant lead a patient into an examining room. To his left was Dr. Smolen's office. The door was closed. Toby walked over, raised his hand to knock. He wanted to ask Dr. Smolen if he was going to need surgery. He held his hand ready to knock as he heard Dr. Smolen's voice on the phone.

"Yes, Mrs. McGuire, I know this is serious, but it's out of my field. This is not a dental problem... Oh, you found the tape? Nothing, huh. That's what I saw, too. Listen, I have a colleague who's a child psychologist. I think you need to make an appointment right away. Let me give you his number."

"I'm not crazy!" Toby screamed. He ran down the hallway. People came out of side offices as he ran. He heard Dr. Smolen behind him.

"Wait, Toby! I can help you! Gingrich, don't let him get out the door!"

As Toby rounded the receptionist's desk, a big, burly lab technician lunged to block the front door. But, compared to Toby, he moved in slow motion. Toby burst through the door and ran through the parking lot.

"Toby!" yelled Dr. Smolen.

Toby glanced back. They were still chasing him. He cut across the street between two parked cars. He heard a squeal of tires, then he lost track of time.

He opened his eyes to the blue sky. He blinked. He seemed to be lying on the pavement. It was hot. He tried to get up, but his legs wouldn't work. He raised his head.

Dr. Smolen bent over him. "Don't worry, Toby, everything's going to be fine."

He didn't believe that. He heard a distant siren getting closer. Dr. Smolen disappeared. The wigglers came out to play with his tongue. He closed his eyes and laid his head back onto the pavement. He wondered what would happen if he could get them between his teeth and bite them off. He felt a sharp pain in his teeth. Okay, I get it, guys. No biting. He passed out.

Toby opened his eyes as if from a long, hard sleep. He ached all over. His nose itched. When he tried to scratch, his hand wouldn't work. He tried his other hand. It, too, refused to budge. As the fog lifted from his vision, he saw his hands lying by his side. They were strapped down. One of his legs was in a cast and hanging from some kind of contraption.

He panicked. He strained against the straps. The wigglers were going crazy, lashing against his tongue and the roof of his mouth.

"Go away! Can't you see I'm busy?"

It was no use; his arms wouldn't move.

"He's awake," someone said.

His mother, father, and sister came into view, concern chiseled into their features. The wigglers withdrew.

"Where am I?"

"You're in a hospital, Son," said his dad. "You took a pretty bad hit from a car. Uh, who were you talking to, just now?"

Toby smiled crookedly. "Come on, Dad. I know you know the story by now. The Dentist told Mom and Mom told you. Or Marty told you."

"I had to tell," said Marty. "You're not well. And I don't mean just the car accident... "

"Shush," said his mother. "Toby, I know you think you have these, uh, things in your mouth-"

"I call them wigglers," said Toby. "You want to see them? Look!"

He held his mouth open, knowing full well they wouldn't show themselves.

"Toby-" began his mother.

"I know. You can't see them. I told you-" he raised his voice, "-I told everyone who will listen, THEY DON'T WANT TO BE SEEN! Except by me, of course. They love to show off for me."

His face contorted and tears streamed from his eyes, washing away the bravado. "Mom. Dad. Marty." He looked at each of them in turn. "You've got to help me. They're driving me crazy. I don't want to go crazy."

They patted him, tried to console him.

"The only thing I know," he sobbed, "is that they hide when people are around me. They want me to themselves. From now on, I want to always be around someone and I'm going to keep my mouth open as much as possible so they won't come out."

They hugged him and talked some more, then his father said, "Your mother and I have to go into the waiting room for a minute. Marty will stay here with you."

"Why do you have to go? Please stay with me!" When he finished talking, he let his mouth hang open.

"It will only be a minute, Toby. Marty's here."

"Yeah, Bro, I'm right here."

Mouth agape, Toby watched his parents walk out, his mother softly crying. For the first time, he noticed a viewing window on one side of his room. There was a soft light in the viewing room and a strange man watched him. Then his parents appeared next to the man and he saw them talking.

"Marty, what's going on? What kind of hospital is this?"

"It's okay, Toby, we're all here to help you. You're going to get better, I just know it."

"Hold my hand," said Toby.

He squeezed until she almost cried out in pain.

"They want me, Marty. I don't know how much longer I can hold out." He squeezed her hand even harder.

"Ow! Toby, you're hurting me!"

Sorry." He eased his grip. Marty pulled away.

"Uh, I think I'm going to go get a Coke. You want one? The nurse said you could have a Coke."

"I don't want anything. You don't have to get anything right now. Stay with me, Marty."

"I'll be right back, Toby. Really." She backed out of the room and closed the door behind her.

The wigglers came out. They seemed to be... happy.

"Somebody, help! Don't leave me alone," he cried, "don't leave me alone!"

-end-

More About "The Wigglers" & Bennie Grezlik

It's easy to overlook chores in life that we should do for our own good. Believe me, brushing your teeth pays off. I remember an old SF story in which an alien commented that humans brushed their teeth in the mistaken belief that this would preserve them. It's not a 'mistaken belief!' It's an established fact. Ask any geezer with rotting teeth.

I live on a quiet suburban street with my wife Judy and three cats who own the house. I work as a technical writer and trainer. Having not yet attained geezerhood, I still have most of my own teeth, thank you.

Many years ago, in a galaxy far, far away, I had several SF stories published. One of my recent stories, "Slouching Towards Bethlehem," appeared in the SF magazine *Black Petals* in 2002. Happy brushing!

The Spirit of the Woods
by Nick Fox

Kira Lang peered into the fridge, trying to decide between a cola and orange juice, oblivious to the soft poof that came from behind her indicating the ignition of a grease fire. When she turned around, she was greeted by the sight of flames leaping from the pot of canola oil she'd been heating to fry apple fritters in. Kira dropped the can of cola she'd just removed from the fridge, ran to the stove, and removed the pot from the burner. That seemed to have no effect on the fire, so Kira grabbed a bag of flour off the counter and dumped a bunch into the pot. The flames exploded upwards, then fizzled out. Kira breathed a sigh of relief.

Her relief was short lived, however, as a black stain overhead caught her attention. Directly above the pot, a large scorch mark marred the white ceiling. "Mom's going to freak," she moaned. Actually, that was not very likely, seeing as how her mother did not venture into the kitchen much anymore.

Mrs. Lang had contracted a rare illness with a name Kira couldn't pronounce that required constant care. Though she was only sixteen, Kira—never having been asked by anyone—took on the role of caring for her mother while tending to the extra household chores.

Her father recently lost his job of twenty years. So, when he wasn't out job-hunting, Mr. Lang now helped take care of his wife. Kira, having a heart of gold, insisted on finding ways to help pay the bills, especially the all-important medical ones, at least until her father could find a new job.

Kira missed playing with her friends and doing fun things like she used to. But her family meant more to her than anything, so she really didn't mind. She just wished she could do more.

Being a beautiful girl, both inside and out, she could have easily found herself a wealthy boyfriend to help with the financial burdens. Indeed, having lots of money could have enabled her family to hire the best doctors and nurses to keep round-the-clock watch on her mother. Money could also have afforded them live-in maids to cook and clean the house. And her father could have gone back to school to pursue the career of his dreams. But Kira wanted to contribute in her own fashion and she was nothing like her older sister, Miran, who had left home early to wed for money. Even with all her newfound wealth, Miran didn't help her family out, for she wanted all of it for herself. Kira knew no such greed—and her love could not be sold.

Kira knew a kindly old man who'd offered her a corner of his table rent-free at the local farmer's market. She'd hoped to make some money by selling fresh apple fritters there, but after nearly burning her parents' house down, she decided to stay away from hot oil. Feeling awful about what she'd done, and wanting to be alone for a while, Kira went off to the woods to find some berries to sell instead.

The woodlands that bordered the residential area that she lived in always struck Kira as a foreign land, or at least an ancient land untouched by modern amenities. So far anyway, since she figured it would only be a matter of time before more trees were felled and houses built. Then again, maybe the area would be protected as a national reserve or something, she hoped.

A while later, when she'd pretty much filled her knapsack with berries, she came upon a little boy sitting on a log. The child was pale and crying. "Are you lost?" Kira asked, worried.

"N-n-no," the boy replied. "I just wandered too far from home, and I missed lunch. I'm tired and dizzy, and I don't think I can make it back home!"

"There, there—it just sounds like you need some nourishment. Here, have some of my berries."

The boy's eyes lit up. "Thank you!"

The hungry child took only one berry at first, but then quickly gobbled up all that she had. The color swiftly returned to his face, and he took off running—calling a quick "thank you" and "goodbye" over his shoulder.

Kira smiled after him, then set forth to pick some more berries. When she was almost done picking her second batch, a frenzied peeping caught her ear. She looked up just in time to see a baby bird, wildly flapping its underdeveloped wings, come spiraling down toward her. Kira only had an instant to react, so she opened up her sack to catch the poor bird. The little creature survived unscathed, but unfortunately most of the berries were crushed by the impact.

Kira was very tired from the day's exertions, but she thought of her ill mother and unemployed father and refused to go home empty handed.

So she went back to work once more.

Later, being exhausted from her extra backbreaking

harvesting, she decided to rest under a tree. Suddenly, an apple fell to the ground next to her knee. Picking it up, she declared, "I'll take this home for mother." One by one, several more apples fell to the ground. "This one's for father," she said happily, "this one's for sister, and this one's for sister's husband." Of course, the apple she chose for herself was the smallest and the last one she found.

Kira put all the apples in her pack with the berries she'd gathered, being careful not to crush them. She stood up, stretched, and began to make her way home through the forest. It was getting late, but she still had time to get home before nightfall. Or so she thought. Without warning, the sky turned from dim light to pitch dark, leaving Kira lost where the woods were the deepest.

The surroundings and the paths she thought she knew so well were suddenly spooky, with dark shadows and weird sounds all around. She started to get scared — goosebumps sprouted all over her skin. She ran like the wind, her feet barely touching the ground. With her heart pounding loudly, she felt that someone or something was chasing her. As she looked fearfully over her shoulder, she tripped on a rock and fell, sending her berries and the apples sprawling across the forest floor.

Feeling defeated and not caring what the scary forest might do to her, Kira sat up and cried at her misfortune, not even thinking about the cuts and bruises on her legs. What was she going to do now? All that hard work and she had nothing to show for it. That's when Kira thought about her family once more and decided to stop feeling sorry for herself. She'd just have to try again tomorrow.

Picking up the less-appealing but still edible apples, Kira brushed herself off and tried to find the path home again. But the further she walked, the less familiar the rocks and trees seemed to be. Then she came upon an unusual-looking dwelling that appeared abandoned. Still scared, and now extremely tired, she decided to seek shelter there for the night. Her parents would be worried stiff about her, but it seemed more sensible to stay safe then to risk serious injury traipsing around the woods in the dark. *And besides*, she thought with a shudder, *who knows what kind of wild animals lurk in the night?*

She'd just entered the odd house when she heard voices outside. The sounds were loud and raucous, which intensified her fright. Kira peered through a window to see what was near. She saw six hooded figures, and they were headed straight for the door. As they came closer she recognized features that even further heightened her fear: Short, furry, dirty, thickset creatures, with evil eyes and sharp teeth.

They were *goblins*!

Though she'd only seen pictures in books, and she would have laughed if anyone had told her the monsters existed, she could not deny what her eyes told her.

Kira looked around frantically for a hiding place. She climbed in a large cupboard, the closest place to hide. She made it just in time, as the goblins came inside right when she closed the cupboard door. They remained in the main room, eliminating any chances of her sneaking away. At least Kira did not have to be afraid that they'd hear the sounds of her heart pounding, because although the goblins were all near each other, they chose to shout.

They assembled around a sturdy stone table, each goblin brandishing a mallet. The mallets were similar, but each had its own distinguishing design. Despite the intricate carvings on the mallets' surfaces, the goblins were banging them all about.

The banging became less chaotic, more controlled, and the goblins' rowdy conversations subsided. Their voices rose even louder though, as they went into a chant. "Gold! Gold! We want gold! Deliver us gold!" Bang! Bang! Bang! They repeated their chant thrice, and then shouted another. "Diamonds! Diamonds! We want diamonds! Give us diamonds!" Bang! Bang! Bang!

The chanting ended just as Kira's stomach began to growl. Afraid her stomach would rumble too loudly, she bit into one of the juicy apples. The fruit was firmer than she'd realized, for her bite made quite the crunch! Kira froze, daring not to chew the chunk of apple in her mouth.

Incredibly, the loud sound spooked the fierce goblins. "The *ogres* are coming!" one of them exclaimed. "The ogres are coming to smash and bash us a bunch!"

The goblins fled in panic, leaving their treasures behind. Kira tried to take advantage of their absence to flee, but in her haste she tripped on the gold and diamonds that littered the floor. As she fell, she nearly hit her head on one of the mallets the goblins had left behind. Kira picked up the mallet and got quite the jolt! Energy coursed through the mallet—*magical* energy, she knew according to goblin lore. On an impulse, she filled her pack fully with the diamonds and gold, leaving the magical mallets so the goblins could make more.

Kira used her riches wisely — she had her parents' kitchen refurbished, paid her mother's medical bills, sent her father back to school, and put the rest away for when future needs arose. Of course, Miran demanded to know how her sister had come into so much wealth all of a sudden. Kira told her what had happened without hesitation, and offered to share her riches. But Miran declined; she wanted more – she wanted one of the magical mallets!

Since goblins and magical mallets existed — for Kira was no liar — Miran assumed that other myths and legends she'd heard must have some basis in reality too. So she believed that the *Spirit of the Woods* had blessed Kira, and she decided to try to reenact the events of that fateful day.

Miran went to the woods and collected some berries. When she was done, she spied a young boy that fit the description of the child in Kira's story. The boy was crying again. Miran feared that he would be hungry, and she did not want to have to re-pick her berries, so she avoided the boy all together. Then she heard what sounded like a baby bird's anxious peeping, but she ignored that too. Soon she found the tree Kira had described, and sat down under it. Sure enough an apple soon fell her way. She snatched it up eagerly, saying, "This one's for *me!*" One by one, several more apples of decreasing quality fell to the ground. "This one's for my husband...father...mother...and sister."

Miran searched for the goblin's lair, and was surprised to find it easily. What she forgot to consider was that it had not abruptly turned dark for her, so of course the broad daylight had helped. After ascertaining that the house was empty, she went in and immediately hid in the cupboard to wait for the goblins.

Miran dreamed of the riches she would have — as much as she wanted, with the aid of an enchanted mallet. She was not the least bit scared thinking about the goblins. Instead, she was excited about becoming the richest woman in America, possibly the world.

In time the goblins arrived with a commotion, as they stomped noisily into the main room. Soon they were sitting around the stone table. They knocked on it with their mallets. "Silver! Silver! Serve us silver!" they chanted, while banging a beat. "Rubies! Emeralds! Bring us all that glitters!" And in a flash, silver and jewels aplenty appeared.

Now is the time! Miran thought to herself. She crunched on an apple as loud as she could, sending echoes throughout the house.

The goblins stopped banging and looked around suspiciously. To Miran's great dismay, they appeared to be not the least bit frightened. An angry-looking goblin stood up, grumbling, "Our visitor's come back — was once not enough that they had to come back for more? Does this fool think we're going to be tricked again?"

The goblins jumped up and searched the house. There were not too many good hiding places, so they found Miran quickly. After the cupboard door was opened, several goblins reached in and dragged Miran to the floor.

Miran was petrified.

The goblins whacked her with their mallets, chanting alternately, "Spin! Spin! Make her grin!" Whack! Whack! Whack! "Fall! Fall! Make her crawl!" Whack! Whack! Whack!

Miran suddenly spun uncontrollably, grinning like a fool. Then, in the next moment she crumpled to the floor and crawled around like a bug.

Then, once more, she spun grinning. Followed again by falling and crawling. Miran's performance alternated rapidly, since the goblins were having loads of fun with their new game. Spinning and grinning...falling and crawling — it went on throughout the night.

At first light, the goblins vanished, leaving Miran dizzy and tired on the floor. She looked around slowly — all the silver and gemstones were gone, as were the magical mallets. Cautiously, she stood up. She didn't spin and she didn't fall!

"Whoa! At least I'm still alive," Miran said, vowing to change her selfish ways. Then she *crawled* home *grinning...*

-end-

More About "The Spirit of the Woods" & Nick Fox

The main moral of "Spirit of the Woods" is that those who are kind and put others' needs before their own will be rewarded, while those who are selfish and greedy will be punished. Also, those who use money for their needs rather than their wants will find happiness, while those who are always in search of more riches and are never satisfied with what they have will never find true happiness. Another moral is that perseverance reaps rewards: Kira had many setbacks, but she didn't give up. I chose to write this story because the messages are universal and timeless.

Nick Fox was born in Ontario, Canada, where he spent most of his life. A few years after graduating University with an Honors BBA, he moved to British Columbia, where he currently operates a coffeehouse with his wife. He can be contacted at nick-fox@excite.com.

"Spirit of the Woods" is his first published story writing as Nick Fox. However, under the pseudonym Nick Aires, his stories have appeared in numerous print and online publications. Nick Fox is currently writing a fantasy novel entitled *Conquer the Throne*.

Taking It For Granite
by Billy Vincent

Vacation planning time had finally come upon Jack's family again and he had been excited.

Well, at least in the beginning, he was excited. As time wore on, Jack quickly became disappointed.

"Where are we going to go?" he had asked. The answer wasn't what he had expected. Six Flags? No. Disneyland? No. Disney World? No. Not even Epcot.

"We're going to France," Dad had said. "Paris, to be more precise."

"Paris? What's there to do in Paris? EuroDisney?"

"Ha ha," Mom had laughed. "There's lots to do in Paris. We can see the Eiffel Tower, go to the Louve Museum, the Arc de Triomphe, and of course the Notre Dame Cathedral."

"Yeah," cheered Dad. "You know. Quasimodo. The bells! The bells!"

His parents laughed and giggled like school children the whole night and their minds were made up.

So several months later they were in Paris, still laughing and giggling, in front of the Notre Dame Cathedral. Mom and Dad wanted to go to the top of the bell tower and see if they would let them ring the bell.

"I'll pass," Jack announced. "Climbing hundreds of stairs is not my idea of fun."

"Suit yourself," they had said and into the crowd they had disappeared.

Free at last, Jack thought with a smile. He looked about the busy courtyard and hated to admit it but it was a beautiful place. The architecture was elaborate and overwhelming to the senses.

"Sure seems like a lot of work for a church," Jack said aloud.

Jack looked about him for something to do. He combed back his dark hair and smiled as something scrambled through the crowd. A small gray and white kitten scampered toward him. It cocked its head to the side as if inspecting him. It then let out the softest meow he had ever heard.

Kneeling down, Jack picked up the kitten by the scruff of the neck. He brought its tiny face up even with his own and smiled mischievously.

"If I took you up to the roof of this place," he said with a laugh, "I wonder if you'd land on your feet if I threw you off it."

With that, Jack tossed the kitten into the air. It tumbled end over end and landed with a thud on the ground. Scampering to its feet, the kitten backed away from Jack. Jack lunged forward and stomped at the ground in front of the kitten. It scurried away in a mad dash and then turned back to see if he would pursue it. Jack picked up several small rocks and began hurling them in the cat's general direction.

"Hey!" shouted a voice. "What did you do that for?"

Jack turned to see a man with a wooden cane limping toward him wearing a ragged dirty old coat. His beard was shaggy and he had a large scar that ran from his left eye to his chin.

"What business is it of yours, one eye?" he taunted.

"Didn't your parents teach you any manners?" he asked.

"Must of left them in my other coat," Jack replied. "Maybe they can tell you where I left them. They're up in the bell tower. If you hurry, they might let you ring the bells. The bells."

Jack jumped about in a hunched over position, much like the hunchback in a movie he had once seen. He chuckled with delight as he kicked the man's cane, causing him to stumble momentarily.

"You're an obnoxious little deviant child!" the man shouted as he stormed off.

"Ha! Ha! Bye-bye Captain Cyclops!" he squealed at the disfigured man. Jack turned his back and doubled over with laughter. With tears in his eyes, he regained his breath and turned back toward his latest source of 'fun'. Much to his surprise, the courtyard was empty.

"Where'd everybody go?" he asked aloud. "Now what am I going to do for fun?" He looked about but saw nothing of interest.

A blue bird darted past him and then began to ascend toward the top of the cathedral. Jack's gaze followed it up to the rooftop where several beautiful statues and grotesque gargoyles covered its ledges. The bird came to rest on the shoulder of one of the largest winged monstrosities.

"Darn," Jack grumbled. He knew he couldn't hit the bird

at that height. "What are you lookin' at, stone snout!" he shouted at the glaring stone brute.

Dust, dirt, and small pieces of stone began to fall as the gargoyle turned its head to face Jack. It slowly moved into a low crouch like a cat about to pounce on a mouse.

Jack looked about, hoping someone else saw what he was seeing. But the courtyard was still empty except for him. He looked back skyward and found the stone cold stare of the gargoyle upon him. Jack's mind had barely registered the stare before the rocky form of the creature was descending upon him, its clawed hands extended. He began to stutter-step backward, trying to move out of its path and keep his eye on the creature at the same time.

The grotesque monster landed like a ton of bricks in the middle of Jack's chest, knocking the wind out of him. Jack and the monster crashed to the ground in a pile of arms and legs.

Before he could regain his thoughts or his breath, he was dragged to his feet by the enormous arms of the living statue. Its cold claws wrapped around his throat and the beast picked him up off the ground.

"Ha. Puny human," he snarled. "I have watched you from above and I am disgusted with your vile displays, your lack of compassion. You lash out and hurt others with your words and actions."

Jack kicked at the stone-like chest of the gargoyle but he didn't budge. It only laughed harder. An instant later, Jack was laying on his back on the ground.

"You are no match for me," the gargoyle announced. "I have not left my perch on high for the mere purpose of assaulting you. I have come to you in hopes of changing your outlook and maybe help you make amends."

"You have a funny way of helping," Jack said as he crawled to his knees.

The beast snarled again and his eyes became blood red. It took several long deep breaths and then seemed to calm. "Now that I have your attention, I am known as Drago," he stated. He then extended his hand to Jack. Jack looked at it and slowly, cautiously, took it. Drago barely flexed his arm muscle, and Jack was hauled to his feet.

"I'm...uh..." Jack stammered.

"Jack," Drago said. "Yes. I know. Sound does travel even up to my ledge."

Drago put his arm around Jack's shoulder and pulled him close to him. His viselike embrace held Jack motionless.

"Do you know what I am?" he asked, his grotesque face only inches from Jack's own face.

"A..a gargoyle, I think," he said.

"Right you are," Drago smiled. "Do you know what purpose I serve?"

Jack swallowed hard. "I think I was once told that gargoyles were supposed to be made to scare off evil spirits. Protect the churches and stuff like that."

Drago smiled at Jack mischievously. "Really? That is most interesting. You see we gargoyles were designed originally with one purpose in mind." He hesitated a moment and fell silent. "It was not as noble or majestic a purpose as those you have given. We were designed to..." His voice trailed off again.

"To what?" Jack asked.

"To... detour water off the rooftops," he said. "We were..."

"Rain gutters," Jack chuckled.

Drago's eyes again turned their previous shade of red and he increased his hold on Jack.

"Don't laugh at me boy and don't ever call us by that foul name."

"Sorry," he squeaked, his lungs gasping for air.

"Gargoyle comes from the French word 'gargouille' meaning throat or pipe!" Drago shouted.

"Gotcha," Jack said.

"You see, we started out as 'rain gutters' and eventually we became something else."

"What is that?" Jack asked.

"We have become more than our humble beginnings. We have become protectors and creatures capable of driving off all who seek to hurt our sanctuaries."

"I didn't try to hurt your church," Jack protested.

"No, you didn't," Drago said. "But you did hurt that man's feelings and you did attempt to hurt a small defenseless kitten."

"I was just messin' around," Jack said.

"I see," Drago said. "Where I see suffering and viciousness, you see fun and playful actions."

"Well, I suppose that's about right," Jack stated.

"I think what we have here is a difference in opinion and perspective," Drago announced. "Let's fix that shall we?"

Drago's grip tightened even more as he leapt into the air and began to fly to the top of the cathedral. He covered about 200 vertical feet in a few seconds, made a sharp turn, and landed on one of the higher ledges near the roof. Drago moved out on the ledge to where he usually stood and extended his arm, dangling Jack over the edge.

"Now, Jack my boy," Drago chuckled. "Is this mean spirited fun or is this just mean?"

"Please! Don't drop me!" Jack shouted, his face ghost white.

"Bah! Boy you didn't answer my question," Drago snarled.

"Okay! Okay! It's mean! I was mean! Don't drop me please!" Jack whimpered.

Drago raised Jack up to his eye level. His nose was inches away from Jack's. "We gargoyles protect. Don't forget what I have taught you today."

"I won't," Jack said.

"What have you learned?" Drago asked.

"Be nice," Jack said.

"And," Drago said.

"Gargoyles are rain gutters," Jack continued.

"Grrrr!!!" Drago growled. "Boy, you have learned nothing." He turned Jack back toward the ledge's end.

"No!! Please!!" Jack shouted. "You didn't let me finish. Gargoyles were designed for one thing and became another."

"What does that tell you?" Drago inquired with a smile.

"Not everything is what it seems," Jack said.

"Correct," Drago said as he deposited Jack onto the rooftop.

"You picked on a defenseless kitten and a handicapped man because you could. You never saw the kindness hidden inside them."

"I understand now," Jack said.

"I hope you do," Drago said. "Should I see you do such a thing again, I won't go lightly on you."

"Don't judge a book by its cover. I got it, okay," Jack said.

Drago grabbed Jack and leapt over the edge, his leathery wings directed and slowed their decent. Before Jack knew it, his feet were on the ground.

"Remember," Drago said, pointing a stern stone finger at Jack.

"I will," Jack said.

The gargoyle named Drago leapt once more up towards the heavens and returned to his perch overlooking the courtyard.

Jack looked about himself. Did that just happen? Did I

dream that? He looked up at the gargoyles above him. They were in the same order and places as before.

"It had to be a dream," he said.

The sound of footsteps grabbed Jack's attention and he turned to find the scarred man approaching him. Under one arm was the gray kitten that Jack had thrown rocks at earlier.

"Am I glad to see you," Jack said, moving toward the man.

"Stay away you dreadful little child!" he shouted.

"Wait a minute," Jack protested. "I want to apologize."

"I just bet you do," he grumbled, as he stroked the kitten's head. "I think you just can't resist another opportunity to ridicule me."

"No, honest I don't. I've learned my lesson," Jack said as his eyes slowly moved up to Drago's perch.

"Right," he said. "You can't even look me in the eye."

Jack returned his gaze to the man's face.

"Sorry," Jack apologized.

"You should be," he said

"Look," Jack said. "I've always been a kid that did what he wanted and didn't care about the consequences. But I've had a change of heart."

"Young man," he began, "you went out of your way to pick on this poor animal. When I came to its rescue, you tripped me and called me dreadful names. Now you expect me to believe that a few minutes later you've suddenly become sorry for your foolish actions?'"

"Yes," Jack said.

"What do you take me for, son? An idiot?" he retorted.

"No," Jack answered.

"Just what kind of trick are you playing at?" he asked.

"Trick? Are you nuts?" Jack asked. "I was almost killed by a gargoyle and now you don't believe me." Jack threw his arms up in protest. " I can't take this! Leave me alone, Scarface, and take your flea bitten stray with you! The whole lot of you can go straight to...."

The courtyard was empty except for two lone figures. Jack's parents looked about but couldn't find their son anywhere.

"He probably changed his mind and went inside to explore. You know how boys are," Dad explained.

"I suppose,'" Mom replied. "I wish he'd said something or left a note."

"You worry too much," Dad said. "I'm sure he'll turn

up." He wrapped his arms around her and they stared in silence, wonder, and admiration at the ominous cathedral.

"I must be missing Jack quite a bit," she replied. "For a moment I thought that one of those gargoyles resembled him."

"I suppose it does," Dad said. "I think Jack's a little more handsome, though."

"Yes, he is," Mom said with enthusiasm. "He takes after his father. Besides, the whole left side of that gargoyle's face is scarred."

-end-

On "Taking It For Granite" & Billy Vincent

The moral is don't judge a book by its cover or not everything is as it seems.

After visiting a web site about the history of gargoyles, I thought that it would be interesting to tell a story that taught not only a moral but also told a little history, too.

I've been married to my beautiful, supportive wife Michele for four years. Our only 'child' is Sally the cat. My hobbies include writing and reading.

This is my first published story.

Do-It-Later Dan and the Possum Tail Bones

by Storm Weaver

Do-It-Later Dan wasn't his real name, but by the time he was twelve, everyone — teachers, friends... even the *minister* — was using the nickname. Dan had quite a few friends. His popularity was a little tarnished, though. It seems that every time that Dan's friends decided to invite him to play, their game would be cut short.

Dan's mother, Sadie, could be heard yelling the phrase all Dan's friends dreaded.

"DAAAAaaaan... Do-it-later DAAAaaaaaan!"

It meant that Dan had left another job unfinished, and their game would be interrupted, so that "Do-It-Later" Dan could do what he *hadn't* done before he came out to play.

Dan would grin sheepishly and shrug, slouching off amiably to follow the echoes of his mother's voice. He rarely got annoyed with her for calling him away from his games. In truth, nothing really bothered Dan much at all.

Do-It-Later Dan wasn't bothered when his teachers told him, sometimes on a daily basis, that he was going to have problems making something of himself if he didn't start doing his schoolwork. The teachers were busy, and Dan wasn't a troublemaker — just a procrastinator. He never got too upset at the lectures, and at the end of each year they passed him on to the next grade, whether or not he'd done the work. Dan figured that when he really knew what he wanted to do with his life, *then* he could worry about getting more focused.

Dan's mother and her partner, Felice, tried to encourage Dan to help out and do his chores and homework. They pleaded, cajoled, discussed, punished and nagged. Dan would feel bad and work hard for a few days or sometimes a whole week, but as soon as the pressure was off, he would slip back into his Do-It-Later ways. Dan was very good-natured about the lectures, most of the time. But nothing ever sank in. He would walk away from the table and go to his room, with *every* intention of picking up his clothes or doing his homework...but the Gameboy would peek out from under the bed, uncovered with the first handful of socks he picked up.

"It won't hurt if I play just *one* game..." Dan looked around the room. "I'll finish picking up later." Of course, "later" isn't a time, and the clock soon ticked away hours until sleep crept over him.

Sadie and Felice looked in on the sleeping boy. They noted the pile of relocated socks, and the general turmoil of the rest of the room. They were frustrated. They went to bed discussing possible new solutions and got up in the morning *still* trying to find a way to convince Do-It-Later Dan to do what he needed to do—without constant nagging, which was wearing on them both.

Sadie and Felice were discussing the problem over Saturday breakfast at Denny's when a woman approached their table. She was dressed in a stylish and colorful caftan, her hair neatly contained in a matching turban. She was a very large woman, with glorious dark bronze skin, and her hazel eyes glittered with power and self-assurance.

"May I sit down?" she asked, her voice deep and melodious with a strong Cajun accent.

Sadie and Felice scooted to sit together on one side and let the woman take the other side of the booth.

"I couldna help but overhear ye' problem," she said. "My name is Olivia, and I tink I can help ye wit yer boy."

Sadie looked at her with a sad smile. "We've already tried all kinds of counseling and child psychology. I hope you have something truly new, because we've about run out of options."

Olivia chuckled deeply. "Oh, I don think ye've tried my metod yet. I work de bones."

Sadie and Felice looked puzzled as Olivia drew a silk pouch from deep in the recesses of her colorful caftan. The colorful pouch rattled with a dry sound, like crumbling fall leaves, as she set it on the table. Sadie reached for the pouch, and the woman placed her hand over it protectively.

"I have te warn ye. Dis be powerful medicine, so it be only for de case dat no-tin else can touch." She held the pouch a bit away from the mothers.

Sadie reached out tentatively. "Like I said...Olivia?" Olivia jerked. "Yes, well.. like I said, we've tried everything."

Felice piped in. "I've reached the point a couple of times where I was sure that if I had to tell Dan one more time to re-do something he hadn't finished, I was going to strangle the boy! I haven't, but it isn't because I haven't been tempted."

Wearily, Sadie nodded her agreement. "What do we have to do?"

Olivia shook the contents of the pouch into her hand. "Dees are de tailbone of de bayou 'possum. De bayou 'possum be a sleeper an' a slacker. He make his way slowly, an listen rarely to bein' careful or makin plans. It sound to me like ye boy, he be o' like mind wi' de 'possum. De bones... dey be spelled te make dat sameness showin' more clearly — so as de boy can see it for his-self an' make te doin' sometin' about it.

"Every time de young man use de procrastinatin' ways, one o' ye shakes de bones. When de bones is shook, sometin' on de boy will take de form o' de' possum. Te change it back to human, all he got to do is *one* t'ing — on time, wit'out bein' tol'." She held up a finger in warning as Sadie reached for the bag. "*But*...I tol' ye dis were powerful medicine. Each time ye use dem bones, all de ot'er changes will come back, too, an he'll ha' to do one t'ing for each part what has changed."

Sadie's brow furrowed. "What happens if he doesn't change back? Is there a time limit?"

Olivia shook her head sadly. "If'n he were te change all de way, dere would be very little chance o' changin' him back. He's got te want te change, and ifn' he don', no amount o' cajolin' is gonna bring on de change. He's got te be diligent in de heart. De bones will know."

Sadie's hands shook as she took the bag, but she was at her wits end, and who knew...it might work. She looked up to ask Olivia what opossums ate, just in case, but the woman was gone.

Sadie and Felice returned home. They sat Dan down and explained all that Olivia had told them and showed him the pouch of bones.

"You don't really believe those things are going to *do* anything, do you, Mom? Do *you*, Felice?"

Sadie and Felice exchanged looks. They'd always been honest with Dan, but maybe he needed to think they believed for the project to work. In the end, though, they were honest, as they'd always been.

"No, Dan. We don't believe in magic, and we don't believe the bones are going to turn you into an opossum if you don't do your work. But this is a sign of how frustrated we are." Sadie looked Dan in the eyes. It seemed to her that there was understanding there.

Dan looked at his moms. "I understand. I know I'm frustrating, and I *do* try. I just can't seem to keep it up. I'll try harder, so that you don't have to use the bones—just in case." And he chuckled as he disappeared into his room.

Sadie and Felice looked at each other and sighed.

Dan *did* try—for about a day. Sadie and Felice saw him the following afternoon, coming back from the swimming pool. When Felice asked him about that evening's homework, he shrugged.

"I'll do it in a little while," he said.

When they walked in the door, they nearly tripped over Dan's boots in the doorway. They noticed that the dishes were still piled in the sink from the previous evening's meal. Sadie knew Felice had told Dan before they left for work that the dishes needed to be done right after school (since, of course, he hadn't done them the night before like he was supposed to.)

Frustrated beyond anger, Sadie's throat got tight, and she grabbed for the silk bag of bones, looked Dan in the eye and shook the bones in his face. Dan's face turned beet red and he let out a yelp. Suddenly, the red of his cheeks turned pale, then slightly green and out of the waistband of his pants, a fleshy tail appeared.

"MOOooooooom! GET RID OF THIS THING!!!!!"

Sadie stood there, flabbergasted. Felice looked at Dan, the tail, and back at Dan. Dan was bouncing around the living room, pulling on the tail trying to yank it off, and yelping and moaning. Sadie stood, eyes glazed, not really watching anything. It was Felice who got her voice back first. She caught Dan by the arm to stop his wild trip through the living room and looked him straight in the eye.

"You want to get rid of the tail? In order to do that, you have to do *one* project that you've been assigned. It has to be done right and on time, and without your mom or me having to tell you, remind you, or nag you. Remember... the woman who gave us the bones said the bones would know when you put your heart into it."

That night, the after-dinner dishes were done promptly—right down to the floors and countertops. Sadie and Felice didn't have to say a word. True to Olivia's word, the bones knew when it was done right, and, lo and behold, the tail was gone.

One would think that Dan would have learned his lesson from that. And he did—for a couple of weeks. But old habits die hard, and soon he'd brought his mothers back to the point of frustration and out came the bones.

This time, the tail sprouted again, but on top of the tail, a pair of small, pointy, close-set possum ears replaced Dan's own ears, poking out of his hair and wiggling as he got more and more agitated. Dan was *frantic.*

"MOoooooom.. My _friends... what if my *friends* see me like this????" He ran to his room, finished his homework, cleaned his room from top to bottom (even his bathroom, which was getting pretty smelly), and even did the supper dishes for good measure. Fortune smiled, and none of his friends came by to see if he could come out to play before dinner or before bedtime, and by bedtime, he was his old self again.

Sadie and Felice hoped this would be the last time they would have to use the bones. Sadie was even getting a little scared. She took Dan aside, in the hopes that a heart-to-heart talk would reinforce the lesson of the bones.

"You know, Dan," Sadie said, "one of these days, if you don't keep up with things and we end up having to pull the bones out, you're going to end up with so many things changed that you'll have to go to *school* like that."

"Mom, you wouldn't make me go to school that way, would you? Couldn't I stay home sick?" Dan's eyes were pleading.

"No, Dan, I'm sorry. I want you to understand this, because it is very important. If you get opposum parts because you didn't do what you were supposed to, what good would it do to let you miss school, and get even *further* behind, because you were being disciplined?"

Dan nodded, sullenly. "I do understand, Mom. I don't like it, but maybe you're right."

Dan's mother knew she wouldn't really send Dan to school with opposum parts. Who knew what kind of permanent damage it would do—not to mention the fact that Dan's father would probably have a *fit.*

Sadie was saved from having to deal with the thought of a half-opposum Dan and school immediately, though. Dan did truly seem to understand the lesson of the bones. His grades started to improve, and he liked being able to find things easily in his cleaner room.

Unfortunately, Dan's motivation didn't last more than a month. Like a true opposum, he seemed to have difficulty remembering lessons learned from one week to the next. He continued to procrastinate and the 'lessons' lasted shorter and shorter periods, with the time spent in correcting the changes becoming longer and longer. Dan lost an entire weekend to restoring himself from having a tail, ears, muzzle and tiny little possum forehands. The bones had become a regular part of his life. Dan started missing school because it took more than a single night, or even two nights, to do everything he needed to do in order to change himself back and Sadie, in the end, didn't have the heart to make him face the ridicule of his friends and face the impact that it could have with Childrens' Social Services if she'd sent him.

The changes got harder and harder. An opossum couldn't do some of the things that a person could, so Sadie and Felice had to make up new assignments that an opossum *could* do, until he had changed enough to be able to do his regular chores.

Sadie was becoming nervous, as less and less of Dan remained after the changes. She talked with Felice.

"I don't feel comfortable with the bones anymore. I'm afraid that one day there will be nothing left of Dan," Sadie said to her partner.

Felice shook her head. "I've had the same concerns. I remember that that Olivia woman said that a change back from full opossum would be almost impossible. Maybe he's learned the lesson well enough that we won't have to use them anymore."

"I don't think I can make myself use them. I don't want to lose my son completely," and Sadie began to cry.

Felice held her. "I don't think that Dan will push us. He knows how far it's gone. I'm sure he's learned his lesson. Let's go back to just reminding him, and only use the bones as a sort of memory aid, ok?"

Sadie nodded and wiped her eyes and went to talk to Dan.

At first, Dan kept his promises. He kept his room up, at least as well as one could expect of a teenager. He did the dishes and took out the garbage, and sometimes even did it without being reminded. But slowly, he began to forget. Somehow, he didn't seem to be able to get the "Do-It-Later" out of his system.

One day, after several days running where his chores hadn't been completed, Sadie came home to find his books, backpack, shoes and coat scattered in whirlwind fashion about the living room. She headed for Dan's room to put him to task and as she passed the kitchen, she saw the dishes piled, undone, in the sink. She found him in his room, headphones blaring loudly enough for her to hear the song that was playing. His attention was completely consumed by the video game screen that he was playing, so that he didn't hear or see Sadie come in the room. He looked up, startled, then sheepish, when she planted herself in front of him, hands on her hips and scowl furrowing her brow. He slid the headphones off and the pounding music briefly beat around them until he hit the switch on the tape player.

"Where are your school things, Dan?" Sadie said, very quietly in the sudden silence.

"UUmmm. I dunno. The living room, I guess," Dan answered.

"Is your homework done?"

"Uh... no... I was going to do it in a little bit."

"Dan, it's starting again. Do I have to get the bones out again? I thought you'd learned your lesson. I'm *very* disappointed!" Sadie looked at her son. He could tell from her eyes, and the quiet tone of her voice, that she was a *lot* angrier than she was trying to let on.

"No, Mom. You don't need to get the bones. I was going to take care of everything, but Jamie let me borrow this game, and, well... I really wanted to play it, and..."

"No more excuses, Dan. You're lucky I didn't get the bones when I saw the mess you left in the living room. I've had to tell you almost daily to put your things away after school and take care of homework and chores *before* playtime. You can't tell me you didn't know better!"

Dan hung his head for a moment. He didn't think his mom would really *use* the bones again—after all, she hadn't used them in weeks, and the last time had been awfully hard to work back from, because there was so much opossum. He knew his mom, and knew that she wouldn't risk turning him all the way. "I'll take care of it in just a second, Mom, ok? Just let me put this game away so that I don't lose my place." He looked up at her and gave her a pleading half-smile.

Sadie sighed. "Ok. I have to pick Felice up from work and go to the store. Just make sure it's picked up when I get home—oh, and there's no way I can cook in that kitchen like that, so if you want dinner, make sure the dishes are done, too." Sadie turned and headed for the front door.

Dan heard the door close and the car start. He picked up the game and did some quick calculations. If he played for just a half hour more, he figured he'd have *plenty* of time to pick up the living room and do the dishes, and be working on his homework when his mom and Felice got home.

It is a true statement that time moves more quickly when you're having fun, and before he knew it, he heard the crunch of gravel and the sound of the car engine in the drive. Dan dropped the game and ran for the living room and started to gather his things.

He *knew* his mom would be furious. He rushed through, picking up papers and books as he heard the doorknob turn.

Sadie came in, her arms full of tall paper grocery bags. She saw the disarray of the living room around the bags and glared at Dan, who muttered an "I'm sorry, Mom," as he scrambled to pick up his coat. Sadie headed for the pass-through counter for the kitchen to set down her bags, but her foot landed on one of Dan's boots. The grocery bags went flying as she tried to regain her balance. She grabbed for the counter and tripped on the other boot, turning her ankle with a snapping sound. Without thinking, angry and in pain, she grabbed for the bag of bones on the shelves next to the pass-through and shook them in Dan's face threateningly, meaning to warn him about their presence and her threat. Unfortunately, she sat down hard as the shaken bones did their work, and within moments there was nothing left of Dan but a pair of hazel-blue eyes peering out of the sharp-nosed possum face.

Sadie blinked, tears rushing to her eyes, just as Felice opened the door to come in from the car, her own arms full of grocery bags. Felice propped the door for just a moment with her hip, so she could get inside, and Dan the 'possum ran out, right between her legs. Sadie hollered after him, pulling herself up and trying to support her weight to get to the door. She watched as he kept right on running. He ran straight for the greenbelt in the middle of the neighborhood.

Felice came up beside Sadie, putting an arm around her waist to help support her. She shook her head as she watched the boy-turned-opossum running into the woods of the greenbelt. Sadie had begun to sob uncontrollably as her son disappeared into the deepening twilight.

"He's not coming back, is he, Felice?" Sadie sobbed.

"Sadie," Felice said. "Dan made a choice. He could have done what he was supposed to, and he could have learned from all the other times he had to go through the changes. I think he decided it was too much work to stay a person. In this form, nobody will expect more from him than he's willing to do."

Sadie nodded and gulped. "I only hope that he remembers to be careful crossing the road at night."

So, children, the moral of the story is: It never pays to procrastinate. The next time you're riding in the car and you see some 'possum dead on the side of the road, all I can say is — I really hope Dan learned *one* lesson and that 'possum road hump wasn't Do-It-Later Dan.

-end-

About "Do-It-Later-Dan and the Possum Tail Bones" & Storm Weaver

The primary moral of the story is not to let procrastination cost you your success in life. Myself and my children — in particular my oldest son — were the inspiration for this story. We have a family history of procrastination, and the family curse is "Do It Later" Syndrome. It's taken me almost forty years to figure out that procrastination doesn't work. I don't want my kids, or the kids who will be sharing in these stories, to have to wait until they're forty to realize that they have a problem with getting things done promptly.

The second moral is about giving up on your life when it gets too hard. I've watched a lot of people give up on their lives and their dreams because it was too difficult for them to look at where the challenges could take them. I'm a strong believer in keeping on, even when it looks like you're not going anywhere. I've wanted to quit a lot of times. Now, I'm glad that I kept going even though I thought it was too much to handle. I'm glad for me, glad for my partner, glad for my kids — and glad for all the people that I'll be able to share with now, that I would have missed the chance to get to know if I'd given up on my life when it was rough.

Procrastination means it took me twenty years to get my doctorate in Comparative Religions, but I finally *did* manage to finish my thesis, and have my doctorate, along with one in metaphysics, one in naturopathy, and one in divinity. I love to talk and teach, and now I'll get to try my hand at sharing all the things I've learned with others. I am happily partnered for the last six years to Aspen, after thirteen years of not-completely-unpleasant marriage to a good man who just wasn't quite a good fit for me. I have four incredible children — three by birth and one by partnering.

My writing credits include old non-fiction sales to midwifery journals on midwifery and holistic health practices, a non-fiction sale to Sandmutopian Guardian on safe pregnancy practices; a novel, *Long Walk Home*, sold in 1999 to Chalice Flame, a small and now non-existant press; and this — my first young adult short story!

Martin and the Mastiff

by Robert D. Brown

Martin loved animals, and always had. He loved other things as well, like the comfort of his grandmother's lap and the time he spent with his dad at the ballpark, but somehow he always preferred little animals better. Whether they were finned or furred or scaled didn't matter, he wanted to be friends with them all. Martin just loved animals to death.

And he had, several times.

His first pet was a goldfish, a big one named Bubbles, with bulging black eyes and a flowing orange tail. Bubbles used to get so excited when Martin came home from school he would swim close to the glass and watch as Martin walked back and forth in his room. Martin loved his goldfish so much he wanted to just snuggle with it at night as he slept, and so he did.

His mother was very upset. "You're still too young to have a pet," she said, "so we'll wait until you're older to get another one."

The school year came and went, and after a time Martin forgot all about his goldfish. Summer was almost over when mother brought home a new pet, a guinea pig named Spots. Martin gushed with excitement over his new pet. He took it to his room to play and quickly grew attached to the little animal. Spots liked his new home so well he squealed with delight, which made Martin so happy that he gave it a great big hug to show how much he loved the little animal. He hugged it tightly, squeezing it against his chest harder and harder until the poor thing's lungs popped.

Martin couldn't understand what was wrong with his new pet so he took its limp little body to his mother.

"Martin!" she shrieked, knowing too well what had happened. Furious, she snatched it away from the boy vowing he would never have another pet. Martin was very sad for a long time.

By chance, one day when he was walking to school Martin happened to come across a stray dog. It was a big dog, almost as big as he was. His mother had told him several times before to be wary of strange animals, that they could be dangerous, but Martin just knew this wasn't one of those. He stopped for a moment to make friends, but when he got close to the animal it ran the other way, and stayed just beyond Martin's reach.

The next day Martin saw the same stray dog again, and no matter how he tried he never could get close enough to pet it. It was the same every day for a week, until at last Martin was able to trap the dog where it couldn't run, and he finally got to pet it.

The animal complained as Martin rubbed its hair roughly, and tried several times to get away, but Martin had cornered the beast so well it didn't have anywhere to go. The boy was thrilled that he finally got to pet it, but in his excitement he started playing too roughly, pulling on the dog's hair, grabbing at its feet, and yanking on the poor thing's tail. At last the animal bolted away, and Martin walked to school feeling great. He was sure he had made a new friend.

That night Martin kept his newfound friend a secret, fearing his mother would be upset. On his way to school the next day Martin found the dog and cornered it just like he had the day before. He pulled and yanked and slapped at it, all in play, he thought, and again the animal tried to run away. Martin ran after it, and chased it right into the street into the path of an oncoming station wagon. The driver just barely stopped in time, and the dog scampered away as fast as it could.

For several days this went on. Martin would scuffle and play with the dog until it got scared and ran away. Each day the animal got a little bolder from hunger, snapping and growling at the boy more and more, but eventually bolting free and disappearing down the street. Martin didn't mind, though. He thought the big puppy was playing right back at him, and that made him feel all that much better. Martin felt it was about time his new friend had a name, and called him Butch.

Then, one day, Martin didn't see Butch on his way to school. Feeling the dog had let him down he moped around all day, hardly ate anything for lunch, and just barely endured his classes until the final bell rang. He walked home slowly, not paying particular attention to where he was going. All the while he kept thinking about how Butch has deserted him. It wasn't fair, he thought, getting madder and madder about it as he walked. "I'm going to have to punish Butch the next time I see him," he swore.

Martin was almost home when he finally saw Butch again. Butch had already dug up most of old lady Bellwether's petunias, and Martin knew she wouldn't like that one little bit. It was the last straw. Butch just had to be punished. Martin marched straight over to the dog, who was so preoccupied that he didn't notice the boy approaching from behind.

The boy grabbed the dog firmly by the tail and yanked on it hard. Frightened, Butch let out an ear-piercing yelp, whirled around and launched himself straight at the child. Martin fell backward with a thud, screaming in fear, his arms and legs flailing against the dog, who was biting at him viciously. Try as he might Martin didn't have either the strength or speed to defend himself, and in a flash the wild animal lunged, clamped its massive jaws around the boy's slender neck and bit down hard!

Martin awoke with a start to the smell of stale linens. He lay there for a moment, not daring to move in the dark, until the terrible visions in his dream began to fade away. He sighed, stretched experimentally, and discovered something stiff and uncomfortable seemed to be wrapped tightly around his neck. Frightened that the horrible nightmare might not have been a dream after all, he opened his blurry eyes and pulled one hand up to his neck to find out what was wrong.

The – thing – around his neck was thick and stiff and leathery feeling. There were some oddly shaped metal parts attached to it as well, like his belt buckle only bigger, and the whole thing was fastened down so tightly it was becoming quite painful. He tried tugging on it to get the thing off, but even pulling as hard as he could it wouldn't budge an inch.

Martin curled up on his bed, more scared than ever before. The dream *had* been real; he realized that now. Butch had simply attacked him for no reason, and this thing around his neck was a bandage of some kind, he just knew it! Frightened almost to a panic Martin cried out to his mother, but all he could manage was a whining croak that sounded odd in his ears. He tried calling out several more times, but the words just wouldn't come out right, and he just knew the dog had hurt him badly, maybe so bad he would never talk right again.

Suddenly he heard footsteps approaching, and a voice calling to him, though through his own whining he couldn't make out what was said. He lifted his head in time to see a man, a huge man, walk into the room and flip the light on. He blinked his eyes several times. He had never seen anybody that size in all his life.

The man drew near, and suddenly Martin realized that this wasn't a man at all. It was a boy! Not much older than himself, he thought, and he was clutching something that looked a lot like an old leather belt in his unnaturally big hands. The strange boy waved the old belt in front of Martin's eyes, grabbed him by the stiff bandage around his neck and somehow managed to hook the two together with a loud snapping noise.

Frightened, Martin tried to back away, barked out to his mother again to save him, and got slapped hard in the face. He whimpered against the pain as the bully spoke again, this time in words that Martin could just make out.

"C'mon, you damn mutt," sneered the boy, "It's time to take the doggy for a drag!"

-end-

On "Martin and the Mastiff" & Robert D. Brown

Children can easily put themselves in harm's way. In the story, Martin's desire to love animals blinds him to the possibility that some animals can be dangerous. When by chance he crosses paths with a stray dog in the neighborhood his immediate reaction is to make friends with it, much to his chagrin. Martin also doesn't understand that animals are not his personal playthings, but should be respected and treated humanely. He antagonizes a stray dog to the point where it has enough and turns on him. Most children grow out of this selfish "I want" stage before they enter their teens and discover cause and effect, but many do not, and failing to master these important lessons early can be an endless source of trouble later in life.

Over the years my interests have been legion, including astronomy, photography, electronics, computers and programming, the Internet, and much more. I work full time selling material handling equipment, and live with my wife and daughter in Little Rock.

My first published work was "The Recipe," featured in the anthology *Bubbas of the Apocalypse* from Yard Dog Press.

Old Lady Ironshoes

by Jeffrey Turner

Ryan and Jacob wrapped their hands around the iron fence poles and watched dark clouds gather behind the Anderson house. No one had lived there for almost three years, and two of the downstairs shutters lay in the bushes under the front windows. The grass came up almost to Ryan's knees, and he was taller than nearly everyone in his class.

"Nate Hanson says he goes in there all the time," said Ryan.

"He's a liar," said Jacob. Jacob was shorter than Ryan but still pretty good at soccer.

"He says he was in there last week," said Ryan. "That's where the bums leave the *Playboys* they steal from the Dairy Mart."

"Yeah, right. I wouldn't go in there for a thousand *Playboys*."

"How about a million? Nate says they've been doing it for years."

"No way." Jacob looked around to see if anyone else was listening, but the nearest people were the Merrick sisters, and they were two blocks away. "Don't you know about Old Lady Ironshoes?"

Ryan laughed so loud that the Merrick sisters turned around to look. Jacob scowled and shoved him.

"Old Lady Ironshoes?" said Ryan. "That's so stupid! I'll bet you think the Easter Bunny's real too, huh?"

"It's not funny," said Jacob. He shoved Ryan again, and Ryan's backpack fell off. "Whaddya think happened to Steve Hoffman? My mom told me Old Lady Ironshoes got him when he went in there and she keeps him locked up in the basement."

"Geez, Jacob, that's so stupid. Don't you think the police would've found him if he was in the basement?"

"If it's so stupid, go inside," said Jacob.

Ryan stopped laughing and looked uneasily at the Anderson's doorway. The clouds were closer now and the sky grew dark early. "I can't," he said. "My mom'll be mad if I'm home late."

"Yeah, right. You're just scared."

"No I'm not."

"Go in then. I'll give you half my lunch money if you go in there."

Ryan glanced at the doorway again and thought of a way out. "You don't have any money with you."

"Okay, tomorrow."

"Maybe," said Ryan. "Come on."

The first thundercloud cracked above the old house as the boys headed for home.

At dinner Ryan asked his father what had happened to Steve Hoffman.

"Old Lady Ironshoes caught him," said Mr. Nielson. "That's why you don't go in abandoned houses."

"Come on, Dad. That's just crap they use to scare second graders. What really happened?"

"Don't say 'crap' at the table," said Mrs. Nielson. "And don't you go near that old Anderson house. Mrs. Ironshoes might put you in her basement with poor Stevie and the other children."

"Yeah, right." Ryan scooped some rice onto his plate. "If she keeps all those kids in the basement how come the police never find 'em? I'd be screaming my head off if I was down there."

"I don't know," said Mrs. Nielson. "I just know that smart boys and girls don't go in places where they're not invited."

"And if she wears iron shoes," said Ryan, "how does she catch anyone? I can run faster than any old lady, especially one with big iron shoes on."

"Maybe so," said Mr. Nielson. "Still, I wouldn't try to find out if I were you. Eat your dinner, and stay away from that house."

Ryan and Jacob stopped outside the Anderson house again the next day. Ryan had hoped it would rain and his mom would pick him up from school, but the sky was clear. The boys set their backpacks in the tall weeds next to the front gate. Jacob pulled a dollar and two quarters from his pocket and held it out.

"No sissy stuff," said Jacob. "All the way inside, for at least two minutes."

Ryan nodded. *Maybe the gate'll be locked*, he thought, but it swung open easily when he pushed.

The grass tugged at the cuffs of Ryan's jeans as he walked up next to the cracked driveway, as if trying to stop him from entering the old house. The door loomed larger as he approached the porch and the hallway beyond was invisible through the dusty glass. Two small panes were broken out.

The door'll definitely be locked, thought Ryan. *Especially if Steve Hoffman really did get inside. They'd lock it for sure after that.*

The cold doorknob turned easily under Ryan's hand, and the door opened with a protracted creak. It sounded like an effect from a cartoon, but Ryan didn't feel like laughing. His heart pounded and his stomach clenched as a musty smell drifted from the front hall. Ryan took one more look at Jacob, whose wide-eyed face was pressed up to the iron fence, and stepped into the house.

The musty smell grew stronger inside. It reminded Ryan of the equipment room in the school gym. He waited just inside the door while his eyes adjusted. A stairway to the right of the door led to the second floor and to the left was a wide, open living room. Further down the hall Ryan saw two more doors, one at the very end, the other in the wall under the staircase. Little clouds of dust puffed up from the floor when Ryan stepped forward. Scurrying noises rasped from the wood behind the walls and thick cobwebs draped the banister. A tendril of silk brushed Ryan's cheek and he yelped as he brushed frantically at his face. The dust swirled in the feeble light from the door, almost hiding a flicker of movement from the opposite wall. Ryan's stomach flip-flopped and he nearly ran for the sidewalk. As the dust settled, however, he saw that that the movement was just a torn strip of wallpaper, not a spider. A harsh, windy noise filled Ryan's ears. His own breathing, he realized, and tried to exhale quieter.

His feet grew heavier as he crept down the hallway. He wished he'd checked his watch – though it felt like eternity had passed, Ryan knew he couldn't come out until the two minutes were up. The light faltered toward the far door but Ryan figured the room beyond would have windows. He stopped beside a hall dresser, undoubtedly used at one time for mittens and hats, but possibly the hiding place for the bums' *Playboys* now. *Jacob'll have a cow if I find one and bring it out*, Ryan thought. He reached eagerly for the top drawer.

Small feet scraped against the old, dry wood as the drawer slid open and Ryan caught a glimpse of tiny, glowing eyes. Something furry scrambled over his hand and Ryan yelled. He jumped backward and felt the knob from the door under the stairs bruise his back. Howling incoherent words, Ryan bolted from the Anderson house. A full block ahead of him Jacob ran for all he was worth.

"You're full of it," said Susie Merrick.

"You didn't go in there!" said Sally.

The Merrick sisters stood outside the Anderson's gate with Ryan and Jacob. Nate Hanson walked back and forth behind them, throwing rocks at a mailbox.

"I saw him," said Jacob. "He was in there for a long time."

"Did you see the bums?" Susie asked.

"Nope," said Ryan.

"Did you see Old Lady Ironshoes?" Sally asked, almost whispering.

"That's just a story," said Ryan. "There's nothin' in there but dust."

"I see the bums all the time," said Nate Hanson. "They ask me if I want some of their whiskey."

"You're full of it too," said Susie. "Bums don't give fourth graders whiskey. They'll get thrown in jail."

"Yeah, well, if he didn't see the bums, he didn't really go in there."

"I saw him," Jacob insisted.

The Merrick sisters looked doubtfully at Ryan. He thought of the two extra candy bars he'd bought with Jacob's dollar and a half. "I'll go again right now," Ryan said. "I'll bet you your lunch money tomorrow that I'll go in right now."

"I'll bet you I'll go in there!" said Nate. "Bet your lunch money!"

The Merrick sisters gasped in unison.

"All right," said Ryan, "we'll both go. We'll go into every room, and whoever chickens out first pays the other."

"You're on," said Nate. Sally Merrick clapped her hands together.

The two boys approached the house slowly, glancing at each other every few steps. Nate stopped when they got to the porch and Ryan stepped boldly to the door, not as nervous today as he had been the day before. He pushed the door open and stepped inside, then turned to look at Nate. Nate swallowed hard and followed.

"What room are the bums usually in?" Ryan asked. Even at a whisper his voice echoed through the hallway. Nate mumbled something that Ryan couldn't understand.

Ryan's heartbeat quickened, but this time he felt more excitement than fear. He walked into the front parlor, followed closely by Nate. They looked at the windows but the dust was too heavy to see through.

"Wanna go upstairs or start down here?" said Ryan. Nate just shrugged.

Ryan stepped back into the hall and headed for the far door. He tiptoed carefully, stopping between each step. He heard Nate's ragged breath behind him and a sniffling sound, as if the other boy had a cold. The top drawer of the hall dresser was still open and Ryan gave it a wide berth. He reached for the doorknob and had an idea. Nate was right behind him, almost pressed up against Ryan's back.

"Wah!" yelled Ryan as he threw open the door. Nate screamed and sprinted for the entrance, stumbling into the dresser as he ran past. Ryan broke into gales of laughter.

After a few minutes Ryan quieted. Now that he was alone again the house seemed to shrink in upon itself. The air grew musty and it looked like the yard outside the half-open front door was growing darker. Ryan started toward it, then stopped as a faint noise reached his ears.

Just as he decided his ears were playing tricks the sound came again. It was a heavy thump, like a bowling ball being dropped on the floor. Two more followed, then another. They came from underneath the stairway. Ryan hesitated, wondering if there really were bums behind the side door. He decided to wrench the door open, take a peek, and run.

He opened the door so fast that it slipped from his grasp and slammed against the wall. He didn't run, though. Where Ryan had expected to see a hall closet or possibly a bathroom, he found instead another staircase, this one leading down. Even more strange, there seemed to be a light on in the basement below. The thumping noise was much more clear now. It drew Ryan to the top step, then down the first three. He crept down slowly, prodding each step with his toe before setting his weight.

The stairway ended at a cement floor. From the darkness around the edges of the basement Ryan smelled the wet scent of dirt and cinder blocks. A wide hole in the middle of the floor drew his attention – the light he'd seen sprang from a source down in that opening. The thumping sound came from there as well. Dropping to his hands and knees, Ryan inched his way to the edge of the hole.

Beneath the floor lay another basement. There was no furniture nor doors, just an open, cement floor. Four small figures shuffled around the sub-level. They walked in a circle with their heads down, taking large, ponderous steps. Each time a foot hit the floor Ryan heard that strange thump. As one of them rounded the far side of the circle Ryan saw the reason for the heavy steps. From halfway down their shins to the tips of their toes, the figures below were shod with great metal shoes. Ryan gasped, and one of the figures looked up.

It was a young boy, maybe a year or two older than Ryan, and his face was sickly pale. His hair stuck out in all directions on his head where it wasn't plastered with sweat. The boy waved frantically at Ryan but didn't speak – his lips were sewn shut.

Ryan screamed. He scrambled to his feet to run for the stairway but froze in place. An old woman blocked his route to the steps. She towered over the boy, her wrinkled face illuminated by the dim yellow glow of a lantern, held aloft in one gnarled hand. She squinted at Ryan with pitch black eyes.

"Hello, Ryan!" said Old Lady Ironshoes. She grinned and the breath floating past her rotted teeth almost made Ryan puke. Tears streamed down his face and he whimpered as the old woman raised her other arm into the light. A pair of iron boots dangled from a leather strap, clanking together as they swung in the old lady's grasp. "I've got a pair just your size!"

-end-

On "Old Lady Ironshoes" & Jeff Turner

There are two morals to "Old Lady Ironshoes." First, the general lesson of minding one's parents – they may have good cause for their rules and restrictions. Second, don't go places uninvited. Kids always want to explore the forbidden, especially when permission is denied by Mom or Dad.

Jeff Turner grew up in Michigan but now lives in Fort Worth with his wife, two dogs, and a large colony of praying mantis. When he isn't visiting conventions around the country he plays ice hockey and works for Microsoft.

His work has appeared in *Alternate Realities, The Leading Edge, The Palace of Reason,* and *MarsDust Online.* His first novel, *Dragon's Bane and Gossamer,* is available from The Fiction Works, and his chapbook novella, *The Garden In Bloom,* was published in 2002 by Yard Dog Press. Early 2003 will bring about his second published novel, and the arrival of his happiest creation, Meredith Drake Turner.

Jeff's website is http://www.JeffTurnerFiction.com.

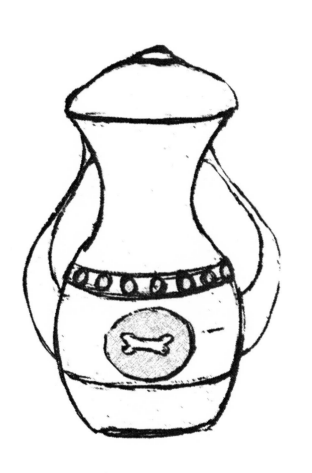

Red, Wolf, and Ms. Hunter in the 'Hood

by Linda J. Dunn

Red turned away when he heard his mother issue the all-too-familiar warming. "Don't you go knocking on Ms. Hunter's door, she shouted when he headed towards the door with his Boy Scout popcorn order form. "That woman hasn't been right since her dog died."

One beer short of a six pack, is what his dad used to say... back before his dad left. Red opened the door and started out.

"Alfred Poindexter Jenkins, Junior! Did you hear me?"

Red paused at the door. "Yes, Mom. I heard. Don't go near the old —"

"Red!"

"Yes, mom?" He smiled up at her with his best grin.

"I swear, you're bad as your father and worse sometimes. I know you hear that kind of language when you visit your dad, but he and I don't see eye-to-eye on that and when you're home, you live by my rules. No trash talking."

"It's on television."

"So are a lot of things I don't allow in this house." She ran her fingers through his kinky red hair and kissed his cheek. "Have fun."

Red closed the door behind him and wiped his cheek with the back of his hand. The things he had to put up with! He shifted the weight of the backpack and headed down the block. Old Ms. Hunter wouldn't be home anyway. No one ever saw her during the week, and they only saw her on weekends during the summer when she was cutting grass or pulling weeds.

Her house stood out from the rest of the 'hood like a nun standing on hooker's row. Hers was the only house that didn't have grass growing in the gutters and plastic covering the windows. Inside that nice house, she probably had better stuff than anyone else in the hood. She was a chemist at Eli Lilly. Big bucks. Never spent it on anything and only lived here because she was nuts. Nuts liked to stash lots of money in their houses.

All he had to do was find it.

Red knocked on the door and when no one answered, he went around to the back and pulled the brick, the duct tape, and the plastic sheet out of his backpack. The guys had warned him never to break into a house in his own 'hood, but he was tired of taking a bus out into other areas and then only being able to keep whatever would fit into his backpack. This time, he might actually be able to take something besides whatever cash and jewelry he could find. Maybe a VCR. He could tell his mom it was a prize he'd earned in scouts and she'd believe him... just like she believed he was in scouts.

Frigging little nerds with their stuck-up brown noses and their stupid uniforms! He was gonna be like his dad. Dealing and stealing. That's where the money was. Smart ones never got caught and he was smart, just like his dad.

Red taped the plastic about one foot above the latch. This was a neat trick he'd picked up from one of the guys. Keeps the glass from flying into your face or forcing you to stand back and throw.

The glass smashed good on the first hit and he knocked out all the jagged edges before reaching up inside to turn the latch and — Shit! His fingers closed on glass.

Sucking on his fingers didn't do anything to stop the blood, so he reached up with his other hand — a little more carefully — and turned the latch. Up and in. There had to be a towel in the kitchen someplace.

He looked around before digging into the kitchen drawers. His mom was right; the old bitch was insane. Her kitchen was spotlessly clean like their kitchen had never been in his whole damn life; but there was a dog food bowl over there by the stove and dog toys in a bed next to the refrigerator.

She didn't own no damn dog. He would have known about it. A dog would have barked.

Red pulled a towel out of the drawer — one with a picture of a dog on it and covered with little white hairs. Best he could do. Blood was dripping on the floor and he wanted to grab and get out of here.

The living room was worse than the kitchen. A huge picture of a big white dog hung over the fireplace and the walls were covered with pictures of the same dog. The display cases contained nothing but trophies. No cute little Precious Moments like his mom collected. No Hummels. Nothing he could snatch as a present. Worthless!

The bathroom held nothing interesting, and the bedroom

on the first floor was some kind of painting studio. Nothing there. Upstairs, the walls on both sides were filled with more white dog pictures and the bedroom was barer than his mom's. Old Ms. Hunter didn't even have any costume jewelry. No coin collection. No money hidden away in drawers. One ceramic bank smashed nicely but spewed out more pennies than quarters. Hat boxes had nothing but hats in them and the only thing of value he found anywhere in the house was that stupid jar on the mantle downstairs. That was gold. He knew enough to recognize that at a distance.

He went back into the living room and pulled the jar off the shelf. Full of ashes. Well, he could dump those out and maybe his mom would like the thing. She had enough junk stuff in the house.

Red heard a growl. He turned around, but there was nothing there except the white dog picture. Shit! He was getting as spooked as a damn virgin. Like he hadn't done this a dozen times before.... Nah! Fifty, more like it.

He unzipped the backpack and gave the house one more go-over to insure he hadn't missed anything. What a waste!

Outside, he thought he saw a white dog sitting on the sidewalk like it was waiting for him. When he rubbed his eyes, it was gone. Must be getting light-headed from the blood loss. The towel was soaked.

Red dumped the jar out in the neighbor's grass and ran water through the jar in the bathroom before wrapping it in that damn, blood-stained towel and hiding them both in his dresser. He'd have to dump the towel someplace later. First, he needed to come up with a good story about his cuts.

He glanced at his hands and stared again. They were redder than usual — a funny shade of reddish orange that almost matched his hair. Some kind of fuzzy stuff was stuck to them, too. Must be lint from the towel he'd used or maybe those stupid dog hairs. Funny color for blood to turn.

Red scrubbed his hands, but it just made his hands redder. Maybe it was some kind of allergic reaction.

He sneaked down into the kitchen and waited until he could hear his mom walking into the room then he pulled a glass out of the cabinet and threw it onto the floor. He bent down to look like he was picking up glass pieces. For a little added reality, he sliced himself with one of the slivers.

"Red!" She grabbed his hand and pulled the sliver out. "Don't touch this. I'll get a broom and then I'll use a wet towel to clean up the mess. What on earth were you doing with a real glass, anyway? You know you're supposed to use plastic."

He shrugged. "I'm sorry. I forgot."

She held onto his hand and stared. "What's this red, fuzzy stuff?" She looked up. "It matches your hair."

"I... don't know. It wasn't there a few minutes ago."

She shook her head. "Well, it doesn't look serious. Go run your hands under the faucet for a bit. If it looks bad tomorrow, I'll take you to the clinic. Lord knows how I'm going to manage to get time off work."

That again. Like his dad wasn't giving her enough support money to cover his expenses and hers, too. He went back to the bathroom and watched water pour over his hands. They itched. Maybe it was some weird kind of poison ivy.

The doorbell rang downstairs and he glanced out his bedroom window. Ms. Hunter. Her voice carried up to his bedroom.

"I want Wolf back."

He leaned against the wall and leaned sideways towards the window so he could see what was going on.

"Wolf?"

"My dog. His ashes were in the urn. I know your son broke into my house. The trail of blood leads here."

"You're crazy!"

"He's cut. He's bleeding."

"He broke a glass. I saw him. I pulled the glass out of his finger myself."

"He has my urn with Wolf's ashes."

"Wolf?"

"My dog."

"You cremated your dog? And kept the ashes?"

"On the mantle, above the fireplace. Your son stole them."

His mom's laughter was loud and Ms. Hunter stepped back a step.

"Lady, you are sick!" The door slammed shut and he watched Ms. Hunter stand there for a frozen moment before looking up at his window and shouting, "He stole Wolf and I want him replaced!"

Red stepped back. When he looked out again, she was gone and the white dog was sitting in his yard, looking up at him.

The damn dog grinned.

In bed that night, he heard her talking on the phone. "I tell you, Rita, you won't believe this, but that nutty Ms. Hunter thinks someone stole her dog's ashes. Yes. Really. She had them on her mantle. No! I'm not putting you on."

He fell into bed, feeling his head pounding in time with her words. His nose felt stuffy and his hands itched and burned. Within moments of rolling over onto his side, he plunged into darkness and pain that had to be a bad dream because things like that just don't happen in real life.

The white dog was there. On his bed. Breathing into his face and making low, growling noises. It bared its teeth and they were dripping blood. Its eyes glowed.

Red woke up and stumbled out of bed. There was no dog. It was just all a bad dream. His hands still itched, though, and he needed to go to the bathroom. He wandered down the hall and didn't flip on the light until he was standing in front of the medicine cabinet.

He tried to scream, but all that came out was a low growl. His face... it looked like some kind of crazy Halloween mask of a redheaded werewolf that hadn't quite completed the change. His nose was long and dark at the end and his hair... his hair was all over his face and hands. Red pulled up his sleeves and it was up his arms, too. He glanced down his shirt and there was fur.

He didn't need to go anymore. He'd gone when he saw himself in the mirror.

Red ran his fingers across his face and pinched himself. Nightmare. It had to be another nightmare.

He pulled off his wet bottoms — that part wasn't a dream — and cleaned himself up. The fur was coming in long and thick, reminding him of a golden retriever or an Irish setter. The color was too bright to be his own.

Bed. Sleep. Wake up again for real next time and everything would be like it was before... except it wasn't. This time Ms. Hunter and her dog were both staring at him. "You'll bring back Wolf or you'll replace him."

He woke up, flipped on the light, stumbled to the bathroom, and stared at himself in the mirror again. It was worse. His face was stretched beyond recognition and the tip of his nose was jet black. He grabbed the jar, opened the window, tossed the jar down to the ground, and then slid down the downspout like he had so many times before.

He grabbed the jar and ran to Ms. Hunter's house to bang on the door. She answered it and smiled when she saw the jar. Once she glanced inside, her smile faded. "Wolf?"

"I dumped the ashes. I'm sorry."

"Where?"

"On the neighbor's yard." He dropped to all fours when

he said that. His hands were paws now and he was shrinking.

"I'm so sorry to hear that," she said. "Did I ever tell you how I found Wolf?"

He stared up at her and she took that as her cue. "He broke into my house when I first moved here. Come inside, Red. Look at what I'm painting."

He trotted into the room and looked around. The living room was just like he remembered except the picture over the fireplace wasn't there anymore.

"Come!"

He couldn't do anything but follow her into that painting room. There, on a canvas, was a crudely drawn picture of him. He tried to stand up, but he couldn't. As he watched, the picture changed from his boyish face to that hideous reflection in the mirror and then.... an Irish Setter.

"You will be a beautiful dog, Red. We'll travel together and you'll win many ribbons at dog shows. You'll sleep beside the fireplace and you'll guard my home from other little thieves until the day someone else arrives to take your place."

Red tried to scream, but all that came out was a shrill howl. There was nothing he could do except... he vaguely remembered something they'd made him read in school. Something about a portrait of Dorian Gray. If he destroyed the picture....

Red leaped, not towards Ms. Hunter, but towards the picture. The paint was still wet, and when he knocked it to the floor, he rolled in it so the paint got all over him.

"It won't work, Red. I'll just paint another one."

Red stumbled to his feet and stood up. It felt good to be standing again. He looked around and saw a picture in the corner with a cloth over it. Unless he missed his guess, that was a picture of Ms. Hunter. Just like the one of that Dorian Gray dude his teacher talked about.

He knocked everything out of his way to get to the picture. Ms. Hunter screamed and tackled him. They rolled around on the floor — she was strong for a woman — until he finally broke free enough to reach up and pull the cloth off that picture.

She screamed again. He rolled to his feet and stood up. The picture was horrible. It was just like that story in the literature book. He grabbed the canvas and broke it over his knee, threw it on the floor, and jumped on it. Ms. Hunter was still screaming behind him. He didn't pay any attention, but just kept beating on the picture until he realized that she wasn't making more noise.

He turned and she was lying on the floor. Her eyes were

wide open and her face was growing more and more wrinkled all the time.

Red ran from the house that night and he never went back... not even when they had the estate auction and his mom tried to get him to go with her. He never broke into any houses again, either, and he stopped hanging out with the gang or listening to his dad boast about how easy it was to snatch things from people.

Paying attention in school and bringing up his grades wasn't near as much fun as what he'd been doing. But you never could tell when learning something that sounded useless might save you.

The woman who bought Ms. Hunter's house seemed nicer, and kids were always hanging out at her house because she gave them homemade cookies and bought popcorn, girl scout cookies, and anything else they happened to be selling.

Red didn't trust her, though. She kept two pygmy pigs as pets... and a couple of kids from his old gang were missing.

-end-

On "Red, Wolf, and Ms. Hunter in the 'Hood" & Linda J. Dunn

I confess that one reason I wanted to tell the story of "Red, Wolf and Mrs. Hunter in the 'Hood," was for the opportunity to write a story in which actions had real consequences. Red doesn't heed the warning of his gang members or his mother's caution and this leads to trouble. When he steals the one thing that a lonely old woman values most, he quite literally must replace it in a way he could never have imagined. While the story owes a debt to Grimm's "Little Red Riding Hood," it also borrows from real life. My husband's neighbors showed dogs and filled their home with trophies and pictures... and a few urns. Red is based upon a certain person whom I will not name for obvious reasons. That individual was recently released from prison after serving about a dozen years for theft, arson, and murder. I wish he'd met Ms. Hunter.

I work as a computer specialist for a government agency and I'm married to an electrical engineer. Thus, our house is filled and overflowing with computer equipment and electronic gadgetry in addition to books. I also work out five days a week and enjoy grass cutting (yes, really!) and gardening.

My stories have been published in various anthologies and magazines in addition to e-zines. You can find, "Blackbird, Fly!" in the DAW anthology, *Women Writing as Men*, edited by Mike Resnick, and "Christmas at Ground Zero," (written long before September 11, 2001) was published in December 2001's *Analog*.

Trank Gun Timmy

by Amy Grimley

Timmy the bear woke up early one bright and sunny day.

"Mom, can I go play with Lunk and Thunk?"

"I'd rather you didn't play with them, dear. I have a surprise for you anyway."

"What is it?" Timmy asked.

"You'll have to wait and see," Mama Bear said. Mama Bear stretched and strolled out of the cave.

Timmy hurried to catch up. "Please. Please," he pleaded.

"Oh, all right," Mama Bear replied. "I found a honey tree!"

"Awright! Cool! Can we bring Lunk and Thunk with us?" asked Timmy.

"I'd rather we didn't. I don't like you hanging out with them. They go to that research station and get tranquilized on purpose. I don't think that's a good thing to do," said Mama Bear.

So off Timmy and Mama Bear went to find the Honey tree. They had a glorious day. They stuffed themselves full of warm golden honey and then took a nap by a stream. Mama Bear was so warm and comfortable that she slept very deeply.

"Hey, Timmy," whispered Lunk. "Come explore with us. Mama Bear's asleep. She won't even notice you're gone."

"I don't know if I should," whispered back Timmy.

"What's the matter?" sneered Thunk. "Are you a Mama's boy?"

"Am not!" shouted Timmy.

"Shh… you'll wake Mama."

So Timmy very quietly tiptoed away from the stream and Mama Bear.

"Guess what?" said Lunk with a big grin.

"What?" asked Timmy excitedly, because this was obviously something way cool.

"The people are back at that cabin with the funny things sticking up off the roof."

"The research station?" asked Timmy with a funny look

on his face.

"Yeah, whatever. I just know that these are the coolest humans. They leave their garbage everywhere and then they poke you with these sharp things that make everything so much more intense looking."

Now Timmy was starting to get a little worried. Mama Bear had told him that it was bad to get tranquilized on purpose. That had to be what Thunk and Lunk were talking about. He didn't want Thunk and Lunk to think he was a baby, or worse a Mama's boy, so he didn't say anything.

Timmy, Lunk and Thunk went crashing through the forest. They came to the cabin with the poles sticking up on the roof.

"What did I tell you, Timmy? Primo garbage," Lunk said gleefully.

Timmy, Lunk and Thunk knocked over a shiny metal trash can with a big crash. A pizza box with a whole piece of pizza tumbled out. There was half of a burger and some fish with crunchies on the outside.

Inside the cabin there was excitement. Voices could be heard saying things like, "Hurry, hurry, get the trank gun," and "Do you have the tags ready?"

The three bears were so busy stuffing their faces that they didn't notice when three humans stepped out of the cabin. One raised a riffle to his shoulder and fired. *Snick!* A red dart was sticking out of Thunk. Click and then *snick!* Again. A red dart was sticking out of Lunk. Click and then one final *snick!* A red dart was sticking out of Timmy.

"Wow! Look at the trees. They all look like honey trees," whispered Timmy.

"All golden and fuzzy aren't they, man?" drawled Lunk.

All too soon the three bears were resting peacefully, surrounded by garbage.

One of the humans said, "Quickly. Before they wake up. Get them tagged." The humans went from bear to bear. They pierced one ear and attaced a red tag with a radio transmitter. Then the humans hurried back inside.

After about an hour, Timmy began to roll around. Everything had rainbows around it. Thunk and Lunk were right. This was great. Moma Bear was wrong. There was nothing wrong with getting shot with tranquilizers on purpose. First you get to eat top-notch garbage, and then everything starts to look more beautiful than it ever had before.

"Hey, Timmy. Hey, Thunk. You guys have an earring.

You've been tagged."

"So do you, Lunk."

"Whoa!"

With that, Timmy, Lunk and Thunk ambled through the forest toward home.

By the time Timmy got back to his cave, Mama Bear was frantic with worry. "Where were you? When I woke up you were gone! I thought you might have fallen in the river. I looked all down the river to the big pool!"

"Back off, Mom. I'm tired!" Timmy snarled.

"How dare you talk to me like that! You are not leaving this cave tomorrow. What is that on your ear?"

"I'll do what I want to. I am not a little Mama's boy anymore."

"You went out with Thunk and Lunk, didn't you? And you got tranquilized," Mama Bear growled.

"So what if I did? You lied to me. It's great to get tranquilized."

"No, Timmy. It is very dangerous. Your Uncle Larry got tranquilized too often and he lost his mind. Last I heard he was caught in a human's swimming pool and sent to a zoo."

"Aw, Mom, he was old. I'm tired. I'm going to bed." With that, Timmy pushed past his mother into the cave and collapsed by the wall. Within minutes he was snoring.

The next morning it was gray and raining outside. Timmy was very cranky when he woke up. His head hurt, and he had a funny taste in his mouth. "Morning, Mama," he mumbled. "What's for breakfast?"

"There is some leftover salmon that I caught yesterday," Mama answered. Mama Bear didn't know what to say to Timmy. If only he would listen. Mama Bear knew that it was bad to get tranquilized on purpose, but she didn't know how to explain why.

"Fwanks," Timmy said around a mouthful of salmon. He finished the fish and then lay back down.

Mama Bear walked down to the river to think for awhile. When she got back, Timmy was gone. *Oh no*, she thought. *He's gone back to the research station.*

That is exactly what Timmy did. When he got there he found half a box of donuts that were covered in powdered sugar. He got sugar all over his face so that his fur looked gray.

Snick! The researcher shot Timmy with a tranquilizer dart.

The researcher walked over to where Timmy was laying on the ground. "Hey, Art! We already tagged this one."

"I don't remember tagging a bear with gray fur."

"He doesn't have gray fur. He just got powdered sugar all over his face from the donuts."

"Oh, well. Let's go wait in the cabin for him to come out of it."

It started to rain very hard. Timmy thought he was high up in the sky floating on the clouds. After a while he decided he wasn't floating. He was lying at the bottom of a lake. The rain rinsed the last of the sugar off of his face. Timmy started to shake from the cold rain. He shook his head and realized he was lying in a large mud puddle next to the research station.

He wondered what they meant when they said that he was already tagged. *I know!* he thought. *It must be that red earring I woke up with last time. They won't give me any more tranquilizers unless I get it off.*

Timmy headed for home. He scraped his head on every tree he passed until finally the tag got caught on a branch. Timmy pulled and pulled, but he couldn't get free. Finally, with one big yank he ripped himself free. He also tore his ear. Timmy still had tranquilizers in his system, so he didn't really notice.

When he got home, Mama Bear exclaimed, "Timmy! What happened to your ear?"

"What do you mean?" Timmy asked.

"It's all bloody and torn where the tag was, and the tag is gone! Did you decide to take the tag off?" Mama Bear asked. "You should have let me help you. My father got tagged when I was a little girl, and my mother showed me how to get tags off."

Timmy felt stupid for not asking his mother for help. "I just wanted to get it off." He didn't tell his mother why he wanted it off. He didn't tell his mother that he went back and got tranquilized again.

When Timmy woke up the next day, it was a bright and sunny day like the day Mama Bear showed him the honey tree. Timmy's ear had started to hurt, though, and he didn't feel like going anywhere.

"Timmy, if I go out for awhile, will you be here when I get back?"

Timmy told Mama Bear that he didn't feel good enough to go anywhere. He went back to his place by the wall and laid back down.

Mama Bear thought Timmy had taken the tag off of his ear because he was ashamed of getting tranquilized, so she decided to go get him a special treat. She looked all over the forest until she found just what she was looking for. A bush full of berries. Very carefully, Mama Bear broke off a branch and brought it home to her baby bear.

The next day Timmy was feeling more himself and told Mama Bear that he was going to go for a walk by the stream. When he got there, Thunk and Lunk were waiting for him.

"Where you been, Timmy?" asked Lunk.

"What happened to your ear?" asked Thunk.

Timmy explained what he had heard and why he ripped the tag off. He then told them that Mama Bear knew how to get the tags off.

"Do you think she can get ours off?" they asked.

"Sure," said Timmy, "as long as she thinks it's because you're embarrassed that you got tagged, and not because you want to go back again."

So Timmy, Thunk and Lunk hurried off to Timmy and Mama Bear's cave. Mama Bear was not happy to see Thunk and Lunk, but she took their tags off for them anyway. She just hoped that they had changed and wouldn't go back to the research station.

When Mama Bear was done, she told the bears that she had to go hunting and asked them to stay out of trouble. As soon as Mama Bear was out of sight, Timmy, Lunk and Thunk headed straight for the research station.

It wasn't long before the researchers came outside. *Snick!* Click and *Snick!* Click and *Skick!* All three bears were tranquilized again.

"Harvey, there is something strange going on here. Two of these bears have holes in their ears where they were tagged before," one of the researchers said.

"You're right, Art. The third one had a torn ear. He must have torn the tag off," the other researcher replied.

"I wonder why they keep coming back here?"

"I don't know, but let's tag them one last time. Tomorrow we move to the station on the other side of the mountain." So the researchers tagged the bears again and went inside to pack.

This time when Timmy woke up, there were wolf faces on all of the trees. He stood up and the fur on his back rose in waves. A deep growl sounded in his throat. The trees were laughing at him. Then the trees were Lunk and Thunk. Timmy sat down, confused.

"Man, you look like you had one bad trip!" laughed Lunk.

Timmy was confused. "What do you mean a bad trip?"

"Well," explained Thunk, "when you get tranquilized it's

not always rainbows. Sometimes things are bad – like a nightmare."

"Why didn't you warn me?"

"I figured you'd find out soon enough. What do you know? You did!" giggled Lunk. The tranquilizers had not worn off yet.

"Did any of you see how Mama Bear got these things off? Timmy asked.

"Come here." Thunk pulled and pulled and finally got Timmy's off. "Do mine now." Soon all three bears were tag free.

"I gotta get home," said Lunk. "My ma will kill me if I'm late for dinner again." All three bears straggled off to their caves.

When Timmy got home, Mama Bear could tell that something was not right. She decided that is must be from his ear. It looked like it had gotten torn open again. She made him lie down and licked his ear. Timmy didn't want to tell her what had really happened, so he let her. Mama Bear crawled over to her side of the cave and fell asleep.

Timmy couldn't fall asleep. He couldn't stop thinking about how bad it was the last time he got tranquilized. He wanted to go back and get tranquilized again so that it could be golden honey trees and rainbows.

The next morning he woke up and was confused. He didn't know where he was. Where did all the honey trees go? Then he saw Mama Bear. At least that was right. He asked her, "Where did all the honey trees go?"

"You must have been dreaming, Timmy. I might know where a honey tree is, though," said Mama Bear. "We can go there this afternoon."

That wasn't exactly what Timmy was thinking, but he said, "OK."

As soon as Mama Bear left to go foraging, Timmy left the cave and began running toward the research station. When he got there, the door was open and there was no garbage. He waited and waited until the sun was going down. No one came out and tranquilized him, though.

Dejectedly, he dragged himself home to the cave. When he got there Mama Bear was waiting for him. "Where were you? I found a honey tree for us, but when I got home you weren't here!"

"I went for a walk," and with that Timmy crawled over to his wall, lay down and closed his eyes.

The next morning before Mama Bear woke up, Timmy sneaked out of the cave. He hurried over to the cave where Thunk lived with his mother. "Thunk... Thunk... Come out..." Timmy hissed.

"Shhh…….. You'll wake my ma!" Thunk whispered as he crawled out. "What's wrong?"

"I went to the cabin and all the humans are gone," wailed Timmy.

"Relax. They come, they go. They'll be back," shrugged Thunk.

"Where did they go? I really need to find them."

"I don't know. Chill. Listen, if you really need it that badly, go charge through a campsite. The ranger will tranq you," said Thunk. "Man, you're shaking!"

Before Thunk could say anything else, Timmy ran off. He ran as fast as he could. He ran and ran until he smelled human smells.

Timmy slowed down and looked around. Soon he saw two human children wrapped up in blankets sitting on a log next to two human parents.

Timmy ran straight at them. He raised the fur on his back and growled. He ran to their tent and knocked it over. Then he began to rip it apart.

The human children screamed. The human parents picked them up and ran to their car. They all got in the car and locked the doors. The mother was shaking a bag out in the car. "I know it's here. It's usually in the bottom of my purse." With that she triumphantly held up a cellphone. "Is this the Ranger Station?... There is a bear ripping apart our campsite!... We're all in the car…. What should we do?... OK, yes, we're at site 39." After ending the call, the mother said, "Kids, we need to sit very still in the car. Don't look at the bear. The ranger is going to be here soon. He's going to take care of the bear."

Ranger Billy pulled up to the campsite in his pickup truck. These bears were getting to be too much these days. This one had a torn ear. *I bet he was tagged by those researchers and ripped the tag out*, he thought. The ranger didn't know if it was a good idea to lure bears out to the research cabin by leaving the trash out and then tranquilizing them. It taught the bears to like human things.

There was only one thing he could do about this bear. It was violent. It looked like a real killer.

Mama Bear had caught Timmy's scent while she was out hunting. She followed it and got to the campsite just in time to see Ranger Billy shoot little Timmy dead.

Little Timmy doesn't worry about getting his tranquilizers

any more. He's now a rug on Ranger Billy's floor. Mama Bear? She wishes that she had said more to Timmy, especially when he started acting differently.

-end-

All About "Trank Gun Timmy" & Amy Grimley

This story is about a little bear who doesn't listen to his mother's warnings about the dangers of drugs. The author chose to write about this subject after seeing the destruction that drugs can create in people's lives. She had encountered adults who first used drugs in their younger years. These adults live wasted lives and can't think past where their next fix is coming from.

This is her first professional sale.

Wandering Eyes

by Brent Zirnheld

Billy had a problem with his curiosity. It had gotten him into trouble many, many times, but he couldn't help it, there were certain things he just had to know.

His newest thing was opening medicine cabinets and seeing what he could find. Billy didn't understand the names of all the medicines he often found, but he didn't care. Just seeing people's private things excited him.

Eating breakfast one Friday morning, Billy asked, "Mommy, what is Preparation H used for?"

His mother couldn't figure out how he could ask such a question. When she had been a child, commercials for the product were constantly being played on the television, however, she hadn't seen a commercial for that particular product in years. They certainly didn't have any in the house.

"Why do you ask, Billy?"

He should have just read the fine print. Billy pushed at his waffles with a fork, wondering why he'd bothered to ask. To find out what it was, he would have to reveal how he'd found the stuff, and that might get him into trouble. Like the time he opened the top drawer of his parents' chest of drawers and found handcuffs and asked if dad used to be a police officer.

"I was just wondering," Billy said. He'd better drop the subject or his mother might figure out he had been in the medicine cabinet at Jimmy's house.

"Why were you wondering, Billy? Have you been nosing around again? Hmmm?"

"I saw it at the supermarket."

She raised her eyebrows in that way that told him she knew he was lying, but she didn't seem too upset about it this time. Which meant she might answer his question.

"Billy, I don't want you going through people's personal effects. You're too old for that. It's very rude."

"But you and dad always say it's good to be curious."

She rolled her eyes because they'd had this conversation before, and Billy had brought up the same point then.

"Billy, you know there is good curiosity like wondering how things work and there is bad curiosity like wondering what kind of things people write in their diaries or what kind of things people keep in their drawers. The second kind is not good, Billy. You are not supposed to bother people's secret things. That is an invasion of privacy."

"The medicine cabinet wasn't even closed all of the way," Billy said with a whine.

"That doesn't give you the right to open it the rest of the way, Billy."

Billy ate another bite of his waffles, but he was no longer hungry.

"Now, you are going to stay over at Brice's house for the first time tonight, and I don't want you looking through their things, okay?"

Billy had seen Brice's house many times, but had never been inside and had certainly never been invited over to stay the night before. The house was huge because Brice's parents were rich. A house that big meant they had all kinds of things, many of which were valuable and probably hidden in drawers and such. It would be so tempting to sneak around and look for things.

What was so wrong with looking? It wasn't as if he were stealing things. No, not at all. Billy had no desire to take anything; he just liked looking.

"I'm warning you, Billy, I don't want Brice's parents to catch you going through their things. There's a difference between wandering eyes and wondering eyes."

"What's the difference?"

"Wandering eyes go places they shouldn't go, while wondering eyes try to figure out how things work and why things work the way they do. You can be curious without being bad."

Billy nodded and hopped up from the table. It was time for school and afterwards, he would be going to Brice's house.

Billy had a strange feeling of excitement in his stomach at the thought of going to Brice's house. Would he be able to keep out of their things? He would certainly try, but it was going to be just horrible knowing there were all kinds of neat items being kept hidden in drawers and cabinets. Expensive things. Maybe even dangerous things.

He looked forward to going to Brice's house, but he still felt a little scared that he might be bad despite his mother's warning.

School went well, and afterwards Brice's mother took him to the mansion. The place was absolutely huge. Three levels high and it had a basement, too. Out back were two tennis courts and an in-ground pool. Best of all, the interior was vast with cabinets and shelves and drawers and all kinds of places to hide things. Billy wondered if maybe the house even had secret passageways.

The only bad thing was Brice's dad. He had long black hair he kept in a tight ponytail, and he was so tall his head nearly scraped the top of the doorways. With his dark, unblinking eyes and haunting stare, he was very creepy.

Fortunately, Brice's father left in his van soon after Billy's arrival. With Brice's mother fixing dinner, that left Brice and Billy alone.

"Your dad is kind of scary," Billy whispered; just in case Brice's mother was close enough to hear a normal voice.

"Everybody thinks that," Brice said. "You'd think he'd make a good horror writer, but he can't get anything published. That makes him very angry sometimes."

"Really?" Billy asked.

"Yeah, when he's really upset, he yells, 'Don't look at me! Get your eyes off me! Don't look at me!'" Brice said. "That's how you can tell he had a story rejected."

"If he can't get published, how is he so rich?" Billy asked.

"Inheritance. His father left him a lot of money."

"Oh."

Billy wanted to be alone in some of the rooms of the house so he could look around, but he couldn't just leave Brice. He had to think of a plan.

Then it came to him.

"Hey, why don't we play hide and seek?" Billy asked.

"Don't you want to play videogames?" Brice asked. "That's all anyone else wants to do."

"I'd rather play hide and seek. This house is huge."

Brice nodded.

"Sure, just don't go into my father's study," Brice said. "He doesn't like it when anyone goes in there. He won't even let my mom go in there."

"Oh, don't worry, I won't go in the study," Billy said, but that was suddenly the place he most wanted to go. "I should hide first since it isn't my house. It'll be harder for me to find you."

Brice nodded. "Okay."

Billy hurried to the second floor, where he found the

study. He could see inside because the door was wide open. If Brice's father didn't want anyone in there, why did he leave the door open? It didn't make sense. What if Brice just made that up to keep Billy away?

Standing outside the doorway, Billy stared inside. Bookshelves lined the walls. In the far corner of the room was a window, but it had been filled with a bookcase, too. The only light in the room was coming from an open doorway. It was a private bathroom.

Billy suddenly had to pee.

What harm would there be in using the bathroom in there? It wasn't like he was going to bother anything, heck, he couldn't even see much with the light so dim. Besides, Brice hadn't told him for sure that this was the study. Maybe it wasn't the study.

Without a further thought, Billy hurried through the study and into the bathroom.

He closed the door and noticed he was out of breath. He wasn't out of shape, but the excitement of going through the study had made it hard to breathe. He had that tingly feeling in his stomach because down deep inside he knew he shouldn't be in here.

Billy looked up and saw the medicine cabinet. He wondered what kind of freaky things a horror writer might keep in there. For a full minute he stared at the mirrored door.

When Billy finally took his eyes off the mirror, he looked around the small bathroom. The tub was large, but it didn't have a shower curtain for some reason. The interior of the tub was a dirty yellow color. A nasty smell came from the tub, too. It reminded Billy of the stuff his father poured down the drain when there was a clog.

"I'm looking for you!" Brice yelled, but his voice was far away. He might be on the second floor, but he wasn't in the study or the hallway outside the study.

Billy stepped toward the medicine cabinet.

Maybe he should at least use the bathroom so that he wouldn't necessarily be lying if anyone asked what he'd been doing in here. The only problem was, he no longer had to pee.

Billy reached up to the medicine cabinet. Usually he ran water to cover the sound the door might make, but if he turned on the water in the sink now, Brice might hear it and know he was in here.

Billy tugged at the side of the mirror, but it didn't want to open. He looked along the side of the mirror and found a latch holding it in place.

"Wow, must be something really cool in here," Billy whispered.

Billy lifted the latch.

"Hey dad! You're back!" Brice said. "Have you seen Billy?"

"No!"

They were close, but not yet in the study.

Billy would have to be quick and quiet. He had to open the mirror now, this would be his only chance. Heck, he would probably be in trouble for being in the bathroom anyway, why not make it worth it?

He pulled open the door and shivered as it creaked.

Billy's mouth fell open when he saw the five shelves of eyeballs. There must have been thirty eyeballs staring right at him! Human eyeballs! Green eyes, blue eyes, brown eyes, hazel eyes. Billy couldn't believe what he was seeing.

Suddenly the bathroom door flew open with a loud crack. Brice's father stood in the doorway.

"Do you know what I do to little boys with wandering eyes?" he asked, stepping into the bathroom.

He pulled a spoon out of his pocket and reached for Billy.

"I take their eyes!"

Billy backed against the wall and screamed.

-end-

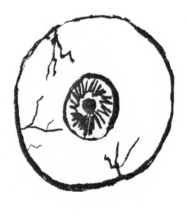
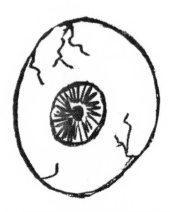

On "Wandering Eyes" & Brent Zirnheld

"Wandering Eyes" is about curiosity that is out of control. It is good to have questions about things, that leads to learning, but when you snoop around in private places you can get into serious trouble and can sometimes get hurt. Other problems Billy had were lying to his mother and not listening to her instructions. Things would have turned out much differently if only he hadn't ignored his mother.

I'm a thirty year-old part-time writer who hopes to eventually make it to full-time status. I am married and have a two year-old boy named Pierce who is very inquisitive. Right now he is too short to reach medicine cabinets.

I finished third in *The Harrow's* summer 2001 fiction contest and have also had a story published in the anthology *Objet d' Evil. More Stories That Won't Make Your Parents Hurl* is my first professional sale.

The Broken Smile
by Wrath James White

Tommy was convinced that his smile was broken. Perhaps it was the loose tooth that was almost falling out of his head. Maybe he hadn't brushed it quite enough. Maybe he just needed to floss. Whatever the reason, his angelic heart-melting moneymaker wasn't working today.

All Tommy wanted was a skateboard. He was eight years old now, and he was the only kid on the block who didn't have one. For his birthday he'd gotten the Sony Playstation he wanted from Dad. Mom bought him the new mountain bike he'd been begging her for. Grandma bought him a Razor scooter just like Johnny's across the street. And his brother had bought him some of those walk and roll skate sneakers. But nobody had bought him a skateboard.

Tommy felt deprived. Every day he watched the other kids leap on their boards and race off down the street while he followed on his bike or his scooter. Sure Sally thought his scooter was cool and wished she had one. And Johnny said he'd been bugging his Dad for a mountain bike for months and all he'd gotten was new wheels for his skateboard, and everyone loved his sneaker skates, but at least they all had skateboards. Tommy was the only one who'd been left out.

Earlier this morning Tommy had decided to plead his case to his Dad. All he'd ever had to do was beg a little and flash those sparkling chips of moonlight between his lips and he'd always gotten everything he'd asked for. But this morning things had been different.

As his Dad sat comfortably in his favorite chair, smoking his favorite pipe and reading the sports section, Tommy crept up on him and flashed him a smile that lit up the room like disco lights. Calmly and rationally he explained the necessity of having the best skateboard on the block. He told him about how everyone had a skateboard except him and that it would make the whole family look bad if he did not maintain the status quo. Not once did his smile stray from his face during his entire pitch. It was carved into his face like a jack-o' lantern. But Dad just told him that if he took out the trash and mowed the lawn he would give him ten dollars.

Ten dollars wouldn't buy a custom skateboard autographed by Johnny Blaze, winner of the Extreme Skateboard Challenge. Besides, why should Tommy have to work for anything when he had a smile that brought out the sun? That's what his mother had said about his smile. That it brought out the sun. He decided to ask her.

Mom had been in the kitchen kneading dough for fresh bread. Tommy walked in with his smile beaming from ear to ear, a smile that could have fried a vampire to a cinder. His mother told him to fold the laundry and vacuum the carpet and she would give him five dollars. A lousy five dollars! What good was that? Tommy wondered. What was wrong with this family? Didn't they want to see him be the best that he could be? How could he be the coolest kid on the block without a skateboard? He decided to see his big brother Jake. Jake had his own paper route. He always had money.

Jake was in the garage fixing the chain on his mountain bike. Tommy walked up to Jake and told him what Mom and Dad had said and how even if he took out the trash and mowed the lawn and folded the laundry and vacuumed the carpet, he'd still only have fifteen dollars and the skateboard he wanted cost seventy-five dollars. Then Tommy flashed his biggest con-man smile. Jake sat and considered it for a moment. Tommy waited patiently, trying hard not to let his smile falter.

Jake snapped his fingers and announced: "Okay, Tommy, if you take my paper route for me for a week, you can earn fifty-dollars and buy yourself a skateboard." Jake sat back and crossed his arms, flashing his own lopsided grin, pleased with himself for having come up with such a fair and equitable solution. But Tommy did not thank his big brother as Jake might have expected.

"Fifty dollars! The skateboard costs seventy-five dollars!"

"You can get a really nice skateboard for fifty bucks."

"I don't want a really nice skateboard. I want the Johnny Blaze Extreme Skateboard Challenge Skateboard. Autographed."

"Then take my paper route for two weeks. Then you'll have more than enough."

"No thanks."

Didn't anyone understand that he didn't want to work for a skateboard? Little kids shouldn't have to work for things. They were given things for being cute.

And who on earth could possibly be cuter than me? Tommy thought.

He had one last person to try, someone who had never ever let him down. Tommy decided to go upstairs to see Grandma. First he stopped off in the bathroom to check his smile. He raised up on his tiptoes to look in the mirror. It looked okay to him. Well, except for that one loose tooth that was just the slightest bit crooked. Tommy decided to brush and floss just to be sure before trying the smile on Grandma.

He brushed each tooth up and down and side to side. The loose tooth started to bleed, but Tommy wouldn't let that bother him. If he had to shed blood to get his skateboard then so be it. He began to floss and the tooth popped out and rattled in the sink. Tommy caught it just before it went down the drain. Staring at his sparkling little tooth in the palm of his hand Tommy felt his heart kick in his chest and his adrenaline race with panic. Now his smile was really broken! Now he would never get his skateboard! He thought about having to wake up at six o'clock in the morning everyday for two weeks to push a shopping cart full of papers for block after block through rain and snow and fog and angry dogs that nipped at your heels. He shuddered. No way! Then, hesitantly, he looked up into the mirror.

His smile looked cuter than ever. His dimpled cheeks framed the flawless rows of pearlescent jewels perfectly. Even that one missing jewel in the crown only seemed to add character to that most perfect smile, multiplying the cute quotient exponentially. This smile was a Granny killer. He would get sympathy points for the missing tooth, too. Her heart would melt down the inside of her ribcage the moment she set eyes on him. He would get his skateboard.

Grandma was asleep when Tommy crept upstairs to her little room on the second floor. She sat by the window in her ancient rocking chair with the sunlight sprinkling down over her wizened face. Her hands were folded in her lap and a contented smile turned up the corners of each lip. The room smelled like a combination of potpourri and mentholated arthritis cream. Tommy crept over to her and whispered.

"Grandma? Grandma, are you awake?"

She was fast sleep. Tommy reached out and shook her and still she did not stir. He was just about to turn and walk away when all of a sudden her eyes flew open and she reached out with her gnarled arthritic talons and grabbed him by the throat.

"What do you want kid?" she yelled and Tommy screamed and jumped two feet off the ground and five feet backwards. Grandma began to laugh.

"Come here you old scaredy cat. Give Grandma a kiss."

Tommy was still shaking, and he was afraid he might have wet himself. Grandma had given him quite a scare. She loved playing tricks on him. He walked over to her and wrapped his arms around her slender bird-like neck, giving her a big hug and a kiss. She giggled softly when she noticed he was still shaking.

"Aw, I didn't scare you that bad did I?"

"It's okay, Grandma." Tommy turned on the pyrotechnics, spreading his cheeks wide in a dazzling display of sparkling dental brilliance that nearly blinded the myopic old crone. She couldn't help but to smile back.

"I see that you've lost a tooth, little boy. I hope you saved it, because if you put it under your pillow the Tooth Fairy will bring you money for it."

"Really? How much?"

"Well, I don't rightly know. When I was a kid she would leave a dime, but inflation has risen quite a bit since then. It must be a few dollars by now I guess."

A few lousy dollars, Tommy thought. That wouldn't be nearly enough to buy him his skateboard.

"Grandma?"

"Yes child?"

"I really, really, need seventy-five dollars to buy a skateboard." He stretched his lips until the very last teeth in the very back of his mouth were visible.

"Seventy-five dollars? Your Grandma don't have that kind of money just lying around child, and not for no skateboard." Grandma laughed again

"Then what am I supposed to do? I have to have that skateboard."

"Well..." Grandma thought. "There's some young boys around your age that hang out by the supermarket helping people carry their groceries to their cars. The get tipped as much as two or three dollars. I bet they make almost twenty-five dollars a day doing that."

Tommy didn't want to carry anybody's old groceries.

"No thank you!" Tommy said with a look of disgust on his face.

Grandma shook her head as she regarded her spoiled little grandson.

"You don't get nothing in this world for free, little boy. Everything costs something. You're a big boy now. You have to start learning the value of a dollar. You've got to earn your money just like Jake does."

"No thanks," Tommy repeated. He left his grandmother's room convinced that he would never have his skateboard.

Why should I have to earn my money? Jake's not as cute as I am. That's why he has to work. But look at me! I'm freakin' adorable! I should never have to work as cute as I am! But apparently his family no longer thought so.

All day Tommy moped around the house not speaking to anyone. After dinner he went straight to his room and sat up watching The Cartoon Network until his Mom and Dad poked their heads in to wish him a goodnight. He didn't even smile when his mother kissed him on the forehead and his Dad ruffled his hair. What would have been the point? The damned thing was busted!

As Tommy shrugged out of his clothes and into his pajamas, he found the tooth where he'd stashed it in his pocket. He turned it over in his fingers wondering how one tooth could have caused so much damage to his previously irresistible smile. Losing this tooth had ruined his life. He placed it under his pillow as Grandma had suggested.

The least it can do is make me a little money, Tommy thought to himself. He crawled into bed and stared at the ceiling, dreaming about the Johnny Blaze Extreme Challenge Skateboard. He thought about waking up at the crack of dawn and walking for blocks pushing that big 'ole shopping cart that Jake used to deliver the papers, up hill and down hill. He thought about standing in front of the "Pick and Save" begging old ladies to let him carry their groceries for a lousy buck. He thought about mowing lawns, and folding clothes, and vacuuming carpets until he finally fell asleep.

When he awoke the next morning, the first thing Tommy

did was check under his pillow.

"Five dollars! Wow!"

He'd only been expecting to find a dollar. Two at the most. This unexpected good fortune gave Tommy an idea. He sat down and counted all of his teeth. Twenty-seven. Twenty-seven teeth at five dollars a pop? That equaled one hundred and thirty-five dollars! Of course, waiting for all of them to fall out so that he could collect the cash could take months, maybe even an entire year. He couldn't wait that long. Besides, that would mean saving each five-dollar bill until he had enough. Saving money was something Tommy was not at all very good at. Tommy had a better plan. He would trick the Tooth Fairy and get all the money in one night— tomorrow night!

Tommy spent all day in his Grandmother's garden picking out stones of a precise shape and size. It was a long and tedious process. There were so many stones to sift through, and his needs were so specific. He worked so hard at it that he didn't even stop for lunch. His grandmother called out to him from the kitchen that she would give him five dollars if he would pull the weeds while he was down there, but he ignored her. He was on a mission.

It was almost dinnertime before he finally found all the stones he needed. Twenty-seven tiny rectangular pebbles. He jogged down to the drugstore and drew curious stares from the girls at the cash register as he browsed through bottles of nail polish searching for the right color. Finally he found what he was looking for. He quickly paid for it and jogged back home, making it there just in time for dinner. After dinner he took the stones upstairs and began painting them.

Tommy stood in the bathroom meticulously painting each pebble with the pearl white nail polish. When he was done he smiled from ear to ear. Then he froze. That would never do. The Tooth Fairy would know it was a con job unless he did something with that smile. He looked all over for something to cover his smile with and finally found some old Halloween candy. He unwrapped one candy bar after another and smeared the chocolate across his teeth until the dazzling white disappeared beneath a film of dark brown. He turned off the lights and grinned into the mirror from ear to ear. His smile was gone. With the lights out it looked as if all his teeth were missing. He checked the pearl colored pebbles to make sure they were dry, then slipped the entire handful beneath his pillow. Once again he closed his eyes and dreamt of the Johnny Blaze Extreme Challenge Skateboard. Only now it was a dream of hope and possibility.

Tommy was certain that, come morning, the skateboard would be his.

That night Tommy tossed and turned fitfully. His dreams were filled with visions of an angry butterfly the size of a small dog, with a big pearly white smile containing literally millions of teeth, fluttering about his head hissing and cursing at him. Its smile seemed to stretch on for an eternity, and each tooth was tiny like those of a toddler. Teeth piled on top of teeth in endless rows of brilliant white. The butterfly was obviously a regular flosser. There was not a single cavity amongst the myriad gleaming pearls shining forth from between the butterfly's lips. It was the most perfect most impossible smile, and it was coming right at him. The butterfly was attacking his face.

He waved his arms trying to fend it off, but it continued to dive at his head furiously beating its wings against his face. He tried to scream but his own saliva kept drooling back down his throat causing him to gag and cough. The smiling butterfly had its furry little hands in his mouth and there was pain and blood and a horrible tugging and jerking that repeatedly lifted his head off the pillow and slammed it back down so hard Tommy thought his neck would snap. It was the most realistic nightmare Tommy could ever remember having, but he was so tired from rooting around in Grandma's garden all day looking for stones that he couldn't wake up. Unless, he *was* awake and all of this was really happening.

But that couldn't be, Tommy reassured himself. *That just couldn't be.*

The horrible dream seemed to last all night. When Tommy woke up in the morning he could barely remember it. But he was exhausted as if he'd just got finished playing a game of football, and his head and mouth hurt something awful. Suddenly he remembered his plan and lifted up his pillow to see if it had worked.

Beneath his pillow was a nice neat stack of five-dollar bills. Tommy counted them and sure enough there was one hundred and thirty five dollars. Tommy scooped up the money and leapt into the air whooping for joy. When he landed on the floor he cut his foot on something and cried out in pain. He raised his foot and could see a tiny white shard imbedded in the sole of his foot. It was a small painted stone. Painted with pearl white fingernail polish. Tommy looked around his room and could see that the stones were all over the floor. The Tooth Fairy hadn't taken them. He hadn't fooled her after all.

"Then what did she leave the money for?"

Tommy's headache was so intense that he had almost forgotten about his aching gums. With one trembling hand he reached into his mouth and touched the tender, swollen, bleeding flesh where his teeth had been. He winced and drew back his hand sprinting into the bathroom.

When Tommy looked into the bathroom mirror he already feared the worst. Even still *his* worst was so much less than what he saw. His smile was now a ragged empty hole framed by bloody lacerated gums. In some places shards of broken teeth were still visible, but in most it was just a mutilated void where the tooth had been torn out by the roots. It looked like someone had used a jackhammer on his mouth. He screamed so loudly that it woke up the entire house. But there was nothing anyone could do for him now. Now his smile was truly broken. Now it would take a lot more than the Johnny Blaze Extreme Challenge Skateboard to make *him* the coolest kid on the block.

Tommy could already hear the laughter and jeers of the friends he had tried so hard to impress. "Gumby", "Toothless", "Crater Mouth", those were just a few of the nicknames he would have to endure until his teeth grew back in. He thought about what his Grandma had said: "You don't get nothing in this world for free, little boy." Too late, Tommy finally understood what she had been trying to tell him. "Everything costs something." He stared at his ruined mouth, and the tears began to flow. One teardrop followed another until a deluge of tears flooded down his dimpled cheeks. Everything in life costs, and you can either pay in sweat, blood, or tears. But you will pay. In the end, *you always pay*.

-end-

About "The Broken Smile" & Wrath James White

Nothing good can come from dishonesty. A lie always turns back on the liar. In "The Broken Smile" Tommy learns the hard way that everything in life has its price and those not willing to work hard for the things they want, exchange honest sweat for an honest dollar, invariably come to a bad end. This story was inspired by my son Sultan Kai who is perhaps the cutest kid ever born and already cooler than his dad ever was. Teaching a kid this handsome and adorable that the world will not always bend to his whim just because he's cute is not an easy task. Luckily he has already experienced the inevitable heartbreak of discovering the limits of what good-looks alone can provide and understands that anything worth having is worth working for.

Wrath James White is a former world-ranked professional kickboxer, a spoken word poet who has performed in venues from coast to coast, a long distance runner, a body builder, and a horror fiction writer. He lives and writes in Las Vegas with his beautiful wife of eight years Rosie, an infinitely adorable seven-year-old son named Sultan Kai White, and two rambunctious canines named Khan and Kenya.

His short stories have been published in the anthologies *Tooth and Claw* by Lone Wolf Press, and *Necrotism* and *Dark Testament* by Delirium books. He also has a collection of short stories featuring collaborations with him and up and coming horror authors Alex Severin and Hertzan Chimera entitled *Broken* which was published in 2002 by Medium Rare Books.

The Empty Plate

by Rob Gates

"Sally, come downstairs now, dinner's ready!"

Sally closed the little pink journal she had been writing in and stood up from her bed with a heavy breath. She looked in the mirror, smiling at her own rosy-cheeked image and brushing the loose strands of lush blond hair back behind her ear before heading down for dinner.

She had been preparing for this for weeks. Her friends from school had urged her on, and she had bragged that this time she wouldn't budge. Tonight, no matter what, she was not going to eat her peas. It wasn't just the peas, not really, but they were a start. She had told her parents time and time again that she didn't like them, but her mother persisted in putting them on her plate. She had been told they were good for her, that they'd make her strong, that she was lucky to have them. None of it mattered, because she was going to refuse to eat them ever again because they were the most horrible thing in the world.

Sally entered the dining room and sat opposite her father. He smiled at her and asked her about her day at school and her upcoming field trip to the zoo. As they spoke Sally's mother came in from the kitchen bearing dinner - meatloaf and mashed potatoes and, yes, peas. Sally bit her lower lip, taking in a deep breath to object but held off as her mother sat and joined the conversation. Sally slowly ate her meatloaf and potatoes, occasionally rolling the peas around on her plate as she cautiously eyed her parents, waiting for the right moment to speak.

Finally, as the meatloaf dwindled and the potatoes disappeared, Sally's mother spoke the words that Sally dreaded. "Sally dear, you haven't eaten any of your peas. You know we've talked about this before."

Sally looked down at her plate, her feet swinging under her chair as she mumbled "I...I'm not going to eat them. I don't like peas." She waited for the response, and slowly looked up under her lashes to watch her parents' faces. They were looking back and forth, some silent message passing between them.

"What was that young lady?" her mother asked in a

neutral voice.

"I'm not going to eat them. I'm never going to eat peas again." She replied more forcefully, her voice strengthening.

Her mother stood, and leaned towards her, hands on the table. "Please dear, just eat the peas."

But Sally would not be swayed. "No. I won't. I'll never eat peas again, and that's final!"

Her mother stared at her sadly for a few moments and then sat back with a heavy sigh. "Well, then we'll never give you peas again."

Sally smiled and finished the last of her meatloaf and potatoes before excusing herself to finish her math homework. The rest of the evening passed as if nothing strange had happened. Her father helped her with the difficult part of her homework and her mother helped her brush out her hair.

Before going to bed she opened the pink diary she had left on her bed and wrote in large, blocky letters:

OCTOBER 5, 2001

DEAR DIARY,

TODAY I DID NOT EAT MY PEAS. I WILL NEVER EAT THEM AGAIN. MOTHER AGREED THAT SHE'LL NEVER SERVE THEM TO ME AGAIN EITHER. I ALSO DID MY FIRST FRACTIONS TONIGHT.

A few weeks passed, pea-less, before Sally began to decide that she disliked chicken. Again she hinted about other foods in the hope that chicken would not be part of dinner. She complained to her friends about how much she disliked chicken. She even tried to hide chicken under her napkin to escape from eating it. But each time she tried to avoid eating her chicken, her mother or father admonished her to eat her chicken. They told her it was good for her, that it would help her grow strong, and that she was lucky to have it. But none of it did any good. Sally had decided that she no longer liked chicken.

It was a few weeks after she had begun her chicken campaign, and Sally was sitting on her bed reading her diary when her mother called her down to dinner. Sally had decided that morning that the next time chicken was part of dinner she would make her wishes known. Like the peas, she'd never eat chicken again.

She stood up and closed her diary with a sigh. She looked at her reflection in the mirror, nodded at the girl with the pale cheeks she saw there, and brushed her hair back and headed downstairs for dinner.

Sally entered the dining room and sat, as always, opposite

her father. He smiled at her and asked her about her day at school and the birthday party she was going to that weekend. As they spoke Sally's mother came in from the kitchen bearing dinner - green beans, baked potatoes, and - yes - chicken. Sally bit her lower lip, taking in a deep breath to object but held off as her mother sat and joined the conversation. Sally slowly ate her green beans and potatoes, cutting and sliding pieces of chicken around on her plate as she cautiously eyed her parents, waiting for the right moment to speak.

Finally, as the potato dwindled and the green beans disappeared, Sally's mother spoke the words that Sally had dreaded. "Sally dear, you haven't eaten any of your chicken. You know we've talked about eating everything on your plate before!"

Sally looked down at her plate, her feet swinging under her chair as she mumbled "I...I'm not going to eat it. I don't like chicken." She waited for the response, and slowly looked up under her lashes to watch her parents' faces. They were looking back and forth, another silent message passing between them.

"What was that? You've always eaten chicken before" her mother said in a neutral voice.

"I'm not going to eat it. I don't like it and I'm never going to eat chicken again" she replied, her voice getting louder with each word.

Her mother sighed, her voice almost trembling in response. "Very well, if you don't like chicken we'll never give you chicken again."

Sally smiled and finished the last of her green beans and potatoes before excusing herself to finish her math homework. The rest of the evening passed as if nothing strange had happened. Her father helped her with the difficult part of her homework and her mother helped her brush out her hair.

Before going to bed she opened the pink diary she had left on her bed and wrote in large, blocky letters:

NOVEMBER 14, 2001

DEAR DIARY,

TODAY I DID NOT EAT MY CHICKEN. I WILL NEVER EAT IT AGAIN. MOTHER AGREED THAT SHE'LL NEVER SERVE IT TO ME AGAIN EITHER, AND QUICKER THAN SHE AGREED ABOUT THE PEAS.

I ALSO BOUGHT BECCA A GAME FOR HER COMPUTER. I'M LOOKING FORWARD TO HER PARTY ON SATURDAY.

A few weeks passed, with no peas and no chicken, before

Sally began to decide that she disliked the wheat rolls they ate with dinner a few times each week. Again she hinted about other options in the hope that the wheat rolls would not be part of dinner. She complained to her friends about how much she disliked the wheat rolls. She even tried to hide rolls under her napkin to escape from eating them. But each time she tried to avoid eating her wheat roll, her mother or father admonished her to eat her roll. They told her it was good for her, that it would help her grow strong, and that she was lucky to have it. But none of it did any good. Sally had decided that she no longer liked wheat rolls.

It was a few weeks after she had begun her wheat roll campaign, and Sally was sitting on her bed reading her diary when her mother called her down to dinner. Sally had decided that morning that the next time wheat rolls were part of dinner she would make her wishes known. Like the peas and the chicken, she'd never eat wheat rolls again.

She stood up and closed her diary with a sigh. She looked at her willowy reflection in the mirror and brushed her limp yellow hair back and headed downstairs for dinner.

Sally entered the dining room and sat, as always, opposite her father. He smiled at her and asked her about her day at school and what she was hoping to get for Christmas. As they spoke Sally's mother came in from the kitchen bearing dinner - broccoli, noodles and beef, and - yes - wheat rolls. Sally bit her lower lip, taking in a deep breath to object but held off as her mother sat and joined the conversation. Sally slowly ate her noodles and beef and broccoli, moving the roll around on the table near her plate from time to time as she cautiously eyed her parents, waiting for the right moment to speak.

Finally, as the broccoli dwindled and the noodles and beef disappeared, Sally's mother spoke the words that Sally had dreaded. "Sally dear, you haven't eaten your wheat roll."

Sally looked down at her plate, her feet swinging under her chair as she declared "I'm not going to eat it. I don't like wheat rolls." She waited for the response, and slowly looked up under her lashes to watch her parents' faces. They were looking back and forth quietly.

"All right dear, we'll never serve you wheat rolls again." her mother said quietly, her voice quiet and sad.

Sally smiled and finished the last of her noodles and beef and broccoli before excusing herself to finish her math homework. The rest of the evening passed as if nothing strange had happened. Her father helped her with the difficult part of her homework and her mother helped her brush out her hair.

Before going to bed she opened the pink diary she had left on her bed and wrote in large, blocky letters:

DECEMBER 11, 2001
DEAR DIARY,
TODAY I DID NOT EAT MY WHEAT ROLL. I WILL NEVER EAT WHEAT ROLLS AGAIN. MOTHER AGREED NOT TO SERVE THEM EITHER, AND QUICKER THAN SHE AGREED ABOUT THE CHICKEN AND MUCH QUICKER THAN THE PEAS.
I ALSO ASKED FOR A NEW BICYCLE FOR CHRISTMAS.

A few weeks passed, with no peas and no chicken and no wheat rolls, before Sally mentioned one night that she didn't want milk. Without a word, her mother took her milk and replaced it with a glass of juice. The next morning there was no milk for Sally at breakfast, and no milk the next night at dinner. But Sally was too wrapped up in the hubbub of Christmas to really notice or care.

Over the course of the next few months, item by item, Sally made remarks about green beans and potatoes and cheese and orange juice and tomatoes and carrots and pork and beef and many, many other things. Each time, her parents merely sighed and the item was never seen again on Sally's plate either alone or as part of something else. Regardless of what her parents ate, and they continued to eat all the things Sally had expressed a dislike for, Sally's plate never included these things again.

Finally, after months of fewer and fewer food choices, Sally was left eating peanut butter and rice each night with lime jello for dessert. While Sally rather liked peanut butter and rice and lime jello, after more than a week she had become quite less fond of them. She began to long for other things. She began to long for wheat rolls, and chicken, and peas.

"Mother, could I have wheat rolls with dinner tonight?" she asked after the ninth day of rice with jello.

"I'm sorry, dear, but you'll never eat wheat rolls again. Just eat your rice like a good girl," came her mother's response.

"But Mom, I don't like rice anymore!" Sally cried, tears rolling down her pale, sunken face, her voice trembling in frustration. With that her Mother silently took Sally's plate, scraped the rice off and handed it back, shaking her head and sighing heavily. Sally ate a few more bites of peanut butter, and a little jello and then sullenly left the table for her room.

The next few nights, Sally came to dinner to find peanut butter and lime jello at her plate. She sat quietly in her chair, her legs swinging listlessly beneath her as she eyed the meager meal and watched her parents eat chicken with mashed potatoes and peas.

"Mom, could I please, pretty please have chicken for dinner?" Sally begged, biting her lower lip hopefully.

"I'm sorry dear, but you'll never eat chicken again. Now eat your peanut butter and jello like a good girl," came the response.

Sally cried and begged, but her Mother would not be moved. She whimpered and pleaded, but no chicken was to be had on Sally's plate. "But Mom, I can't eat any more peanut butter, please please make something else for me." And Sally's mother quietly took the plate and removed the peanut butter leaving Sally with just the lime jello.

She ate a few spoonfuls of jello, then rose weakly from the table and went quietly to her room.

Sally came to the table to find a bowl of jello at her place for dinner each night for the next few days. No matter how much she begged and pleaded and cried and pouted, her mother would not bring her any of the things she had once claimed she didn't want to eat. Finally, in the heat of a particularly woeful round of begging she said, "I can't take any more jello! If I have to eat another bite of it, I'll die!"

Her mother took the bowl from her place and left Sally sitting at the table. Sally waited, hoping that perhaps the game had ended. But her mother returned empty handed and cleaned the table in front of Sally.

The next night, Sally heard her mother call her down for dinner and rushed down the stairs. Please, she prayed silently to herself, please let it be wheat rolls, and chicken, and peas. For Sally was sure that something would have to be different. She came to the table and sat and waited, joking with her father until her mother came through the kitchen door carrying three plates. Sally strained in her seat to look up and see what was on the plates, but couldn't see and was forced to wait anxiously as her mother approached.

Her heart beat quickly as she watched her mother place the plates down. Her mouth watered as she looked at the food on her parents' plates. Then her mother placed a plate in front of Sally. Sally looked at her own empty plate and just cried.

-end-

On "The Empty Plate" & Rob Gates

Kids never seem to realize what they have until it's taken away. In addition, they don't understand the importance of eating a varied and healthy selection of foods. In a world where so many people don't have enough to eat, we should be thankful for whatever we find on our plate, but so many kids complain on whims about foods they've suddenly decided they don't want. I recently had the (dis)pleasure of watching a friend's eight year old son throw a tantrum about not wanting to eat one of his usual favorites one night and was surprised to see his mother make him something else. A couple of days later, he was happily eating the same food he had cried about not liking days earlier. The situation stayed with me and got me thinking about what would happen if a child's parents *really* complied with the whims of a child regarding not liking particular foods.

Rob Gates grew up in rural New England and now lives in Washington DC with his partner Peter. He manages technology projects for a small non-profit organization by day and reads voraciously by night. Occasionally he finds time to write.

Rob's previous credits include the story "It Is Whether You Win or Lose" in the Yard Dog Press anthology, *Bubbas of the Apocalypse*, and the story "Second Chances" in the online erotica magazine *1000Delights*.

Tray Man

by Greg Burnham

As the moving van disappeared down the street Jimmy pulled the curtain shut and sighed. He could not believe that his father had been transferred again. This last particular move had upset him more so than the past three, as he had finally made some good friends and was about to start High School. Another lonely summer was on the horizon.

"Can you help me with these boxes, hon?"

"If I have to." He grabbed some books and started stacking them on a shelf.

"Well I would appreciate it," his mother huffed and went into the kitchen to start dinner. She was worried about Jimmy. He had a terrible attitude about moving and she was starting to have trouble keeping him under control.

As she started to mix a salad she heard children laughing outside the window. "Jimmy, come in here, I want to show you something."

A few minutes later he slumped into the kitchen dragging his feet. "I got three of the boxes emptied."

"Oh forget that, look," she pointed out the window.

"So. It's just a bunch of kids."

"I'm not going to get into this argument with you. I'm only trying to help the situation by getting you to make new friends."

Jimmy slowly glanced back out the window at the kids playing across the street. "Just a bunch of stupid kids."

"That's enough from you young man! What is going on with you lately? You used to be so sweet. I am not going to tolerate a smart mouth!"

Jimmy managed a forced smile.

"That's better. Now get out there and introduce yourself," she sighed as the door slammed behind him.

"Hey, I'm Jimmy. What's your name?"

"I'm Bobby. That's Sue and Stuart, they're twins," the boy bounced a kickball to Jimmy. "You just moving in?"

"Yeah, I moved from Chicago."

"Whoa, Chicago! A lot better then this little bumpkin' town."

"Yeah, it was," Jimmy smirked. "So what grade are you guys in?"

"I'll be in ninth, but Sue and Stu will be in eighth. I don't really care though, we've been friends since we were babies."

"I'm going to be in ninth grade, too." Jimmy started to feel more comfortable.

"Cool. Maybe we'll be in the same class."

The kids all smiled and stood in awkward silence a few minutes before Bobby spoke again. "Hey, you want to go down to the pizza place with us? It ain't downtown Chicago, but its got video games. We were just about to head out before it gets too dark."

Soon after being told by his mother to *not* leave the yard, Jimmy was peddling toward the little shopping center with his new "friends." They spent the next hour playing games and eating pizza, before mounting up their bikes and starting back for home.

"See them?" Bobby pointed to some teenagers huddled around a car. "That's where the high schoolers hang out. Sometimes the cops run them off and they ditch their beer in the dumpster behind the store. Let's go check it out."

They whizzed around to a blue dumpster and flung the door open. It smelled terrible, but Bobby and Stuart jumped right in. A few minutes later, Stuart popped his head over the rim grinning.

"I found three bottles! Sue, run over to the pizza place and get a large cup of ice!"

"Man this is awesome! You guys just get free beer out of here?" Jimmy laughed.

"Yeah! We'll come back around midnight and there will be more I guarantee," Stuart wiped the bottles off.

"No way, my mom won't let me stay out that late, she's a hag!"

"Neither will ours stupid, we just sneak out!"

A gleam sparkled in Jimmy's mischievous eyes. "Yeah, I'll just sneak out! And I can lift some of my Dad's cigarettes so we can have a few smokes with our beer!"

All of the kids started to laugh when suddenly an icy cold hand jutted out from underneath the garbage bin and grabbed Jimmy's leg.

"Something's got me!" he screeched.

"Ahhh! You kids get outta here!"

Jimmy jumped away before looking down at the voice,

and that is when he saw it. There on the ground like something out of a freak show was the most grotesque sight he had ever seen. It was half a man squirming around under the trash bin. He had wild, matted hair with a layer of crud caked on his face, allowing only the bloodshot whites of his eyes to penetrate Jimmy like a knife. The horrid image of this hideous slug, scratching at the sides of the dumpster with his long filthy fingernails, burned in his mind, and if it were not for Stuart dropping the beer bottles and shattering them on the pavement, Jimmy would have been hypnotized.

"Run!" Bobby shouted.

By the time Jimmy looked up, the other boys were half way across the parking lot pumping furiously on the pedals of their bikes.

"Blaaahhh! You heard them boy! Run you little punk, run!"

Jimmy managed to get on his bike and speed away with only the deranged laughter of the freakish half man following him. As he whooshed past the entrance of the pizza place, Sue was coming out with the cup of ice.

"Come on, Sue, get your bike and let's go! Bobby and Stu are probably home by now, so hurry up!"

By the time he got back to his front yard the stars were out. Sweat was pouring down his face, so even the hot summer breeze was some comfort as he crashed into the lawn and collapsed on his back. Bobby and Stuart were sprawled out in similar piles gasping for breath.

"What was that!" Jimmy huffed.

"That was Tray Man," Bobby sat up.

"Tray Man? Who's Tray Man?"

"Well the story goes that about ten years ago he was a doctor, a big time surgeon, but got in a big car wreck and it crushed his legs so bad they had to cut them off so the infection wouldn't kill him. He was laid up in the hospital for a year, the whole time trying to figure out a way to get more legs. Then, right before he was released, they found him in the morgue sawing off the legs of a dead body. That's when they sent him to the nut house for about five years, but he was still crazy when they let him out."

"Yeah, that's right," Stu interrupted. "He got an old cafeteria food tray and screwed some wheels on it and started dragging himself around town like some kind of a freak monster. That's when everybody started calling him Tray Man."

By this time Sue had pulled up and sat Indian style by

Jimmy.

"And ever since it happened," she added, "he has been
snatching kids in the night and cutting their legs off to replace
the ones he lost. The weird thing is that after a while the
circulation goes bad and they just start to rot off of him. That's
why he has to keep on getting new ones."

Jimmy looked from one to the other, waiting for the punch
line, or some snickering, but none returned. He squirmed his
bottom against the grass trying to get his underwear adjusted.
They had ridden up his butt crack during the race home. "So
you're telling me that Tray Man cuts the legs off kids and sews
them on his own body?"

"Check the back of milk cartons at the grocery store, not
much spare room if you know what I mean," Stu answered.

"Why does he go after kids? Why not grown ups?"

"It was a kid, driving drunk, that hit him in the wreck,
but he only got put on probation for what he did. Tray Man was
so pissed off that the kid wasn't punished hard enough, he swore
to use only the legs of bad kids to teach them a lesson. He grabs
kids, like you tonight, and knocks them out with chloroform.
After that he shoves them in a sack and drags them back to an
old house by the lake. That's where he operates on them." Bobby
stood up. "Look it's getting dark and I have to get home, but
meet me under the streetlight tonight at 11:45 and I'll show you
where his house is."

"What? Tonight?" Jimmy looked at Sue and Stu. "Are
you guys going, too?"

"Ah, um, well, not tonight. We have to get up real early
and go visit our grandmother tomorrow. Anyway, our mother
doesn't let us play after dark."

"They never go to Tray Man's house. They're chicken!"

"Are not!"

"Are too!"

"Are not!" the twins chimed in unison.

"Just forget about it. I don't believe all that stuff anyway,"
Jimmy dusted his pants off.

"I expected a couple of baby Jr. High kids to chicken out,
but a Freshman?" Bobby paused.

"You think I'm scared?"

"Oh no, not scared. Just chicken… Bock-bock," Bobby
clucked.

Jimmy started for his house pushing his bike. "I'll see
you at 11:45 tonight. Don't be late."

"That's what I thought!" Bobby laughed.

The cloud coverage over the moon and the fact that the streetlight was burned out made it forebodingly dark. Jimmy could just make out the outline of Bobby as he shuffled across the front lawn, and a sinking feeling rolled in his stomach. It was almost midnight and by kid's law just showing up for a dare and waiting at least fifteen minutes would have proven himself *"un-chicken"*, but now that Bobby had shown up at the last second all that had changed.

"You're late, I was just about to give up on you," Jimmy pressed the tiny light button on his watch.

"Yeah, I didn't ever think my parents were going to go to sleep. So, you ready to go?"

"How far away is this house?"

"Down by the lake, not far from here." Bobby started down the road. "Come on let's go!"

Jimmy sighed nervously and hurried behind him.

After clearing town it was evident they had arrived, as Jimmy could smell the fresh lake water in the summer breeze. The full moon had broken from the clouds of earlier and it shone brightly over the lake, eerily illuminating the dark waters. They stopped at a dilapidated wooden boat ramp.

"Come on, it's just down the path a bit."

Jimmy gulped at the lump in his throat.

As they stumbled through the darkness all Jimmy could envision was the hideous image of the half-man scratching his way through the filth and trash with those hellish eyes fixed in hollow sockets, glaring into his soul.

"There it is," Bobby pointed to a broken-down house in a small clearing. "That's where Tray Man lives."

The two boys peeked through a dirty window into a cluttered room illuminated only by the moonlight. All sorts of junk was piled high everywhere. Old magazines, aluminum cans, car tires, garbage; it resembled an in-door junkyard.

"I bet he buries the bodies under all that crap in there," Bobby nudged Jimmy in the arm, but it was not this comment that made Jimmy cringe, it was what he saw on the wall.

In the moonlight he could make out the headlines of a tattered yellowed newspaper clipping tacked to the wall that read: Drunk Driver Runs Into Prominent Doctor With Crippling Results.

"Oh man! Did you read that Bobby?"

"Read wha... Ahhh! He's got me! Get him off me!" Bobby started kicking and broke away from the window. In the same instant Jimmy felt an ice-cold grip clasp onto his ankle, just as it had done earlier by the trash bin.

"You better run you little bastard!" Tray Man yelled as Bobby ran into the woods. "I'm gonna get you! And *you*," he turned his attention back to Jimmy. "You're just plain screwed, little boy!"

A displaced moistness quickly spread in his shorts before the warm trickle puddled in his shoe, but other than the urine moving down his leg, Jimmy was totally paralyzed. He could not even breath as the stumpy torso squeezed up tight against him, humping it's way up his body, hands groping aimlessly at his clothes, pulling closer to his face with every thrust. Jimmy shut his eyes tight as the tears swelled and knots tightened in his stomach, but it did not stop the attack. He could now feel the foul, stagnate breath huff onto his cheeks. This was the end for sure, he thought.

"Open your eyes, boy," Tray Man hissed.

Jimmy obeyed out of shear fear and squinted his eyes slightly, but when he did the tears started to flow. He was literally nose to nose with the insidious Tray Man.

"Take me inside and put me up in my chair, boy!" Tray man barked.

"Y-yes, s-sir," Bobby did as he was told.

After easing into the dark, damp room and placing the stumpy freak into a moldy recliner Jimmy raced frantically for the door. The tears compounded when he realized it was securely locked. He was in complete horror of what might happen next, so he nervously inspected the smelly cluttered room in an effort to devise a plan.

"You didn't think I was going to leave the door unlocked did you? All my doors and windows lock from the outside, so when nosey little punks get in, they can't get out, and I've got the only key stashed away," he started to chuckle.

"What do you want from me?"

"What do you think?"

"My l-l-legs," Jimmy trembled.

Upon this reply, Tray Man went stone cold silent, and the malicious smirk disappeared from his lips. "Come pick me up, now!"

A frigid jolt shook Jimmy to the core in the wake of the forceful command and only after a few seconds of violent tremors could he manage to get to the hideous quasi-man and pick him up.

"Good. Now take me through there!"

Jimmy's heart skipped as he followed the bony, scabbed finger of Tray Man that pointed at a shadowy doorway. He hesitated, mortified by the possibilities of what was hidden within the blackness, but then a pain, sharp and complete, pierced his side. He squealed.

"You don't take me into that room, then I'm going to push this knife into your kidney all the way through your stomach and then out the other side."

Jimmy remained motionless in petrified fear.

"Don't test me boy, or I'll do a little twistin' and turnin' while I'm in there and really mess you up good!" He pushed the point of the blade into Jimmy's skin slightly more.

"Okay. Okay. I'm going," Jimmy whimpered.

He walked slowly, getting closer to the unknown with every step. He could feel his heart pounding furiously in his chest as if it were going to explode, then just as the total darkness consumed them both, he heard a click, followed by the weak hum of fluorescent lights. Directly under the light was a large steel table and several smaller steel tables around it.

"Put me there," Tray Man pointed to the largest table.

He released the wormy fiend, realizing what the table was. The top was littered with scattered chunks of decaying meat, and at the foot of the table was a drain, polluted with congealed blood and a putrid odor. It also had leg and arm straps encrusted in various filth. It was an old autopsy slab.

The smaller supporting table was covered in rusted archaic tools such as chisels, scalpels and bone saws. Jimmy's feet moved quicker than his mind, and he found himself banging on the door they had just come through.

"Jimbo, you should know better by now. It locked behind us, remember?" he hissed. "Now get your butt up on the table, boy!"

Jimmy searched the room again, and then he noticed it. He could just make it out in the dull yellow light, but it was definitely another door on the far side of the room. He moved quickly past the slab that Tray Man was perched on and to the door. He grabbed the doorknob; it turned. A feeling flushed over him like cool water on a hot day, and he hurried through the door locking it behind him. He pulled the cord on the light and found that he was in a dirty little toilet room.

A small piece of the wall was hanging loose just above a filthy commode that stank of raw sewage, so he pulled at it vigorously, but his effort was futile. He could not loosen any more boards and in a panic started to shout for help through the tiny hole.

"Hey boy, you best shut your yap in there, or I'm gonna rip your tongue out!"

This urged Jimmy to scream out louder and when he did, the unexpected happened. Someone answered him from outside.

"Hey Jimmy, it's me," Bobby whispered through the crack in the wall. "Listen you have got to be quiet so he doesn't freak out on you."

"You got to get me out of here, now! He's going to cut my legs off!"

"Shh," Bobby hissed in another low whisper. "I got an idea."

Jimmy stopped crying for a moment. "What?"

"You go back into the room and..."

"Are you crazy?!"

"Shut up or he's going to know someone else is out here," Bobby answered. "Now hear me out, okay?"

Jimmy sniffed the dripping snot from his nose and nodded affirmatively.

"Alright," Bobby continued. "Now listen to me. You are going to have to go back in there and let him think you've given up. I'll go around through the house and prop the doors open, so when he tries to get you again I can charge in and knock him out, then we can get out of here and call the cops."

Jimmy went silent and thoughtful for a moment then exhaled deeply. "That's a good plan, but hurry up."

Jimmy went to the door and cleared the phlegm from his throat. "Hey, Tray Man! Let's make a deal."

"What do you think you're talking about?" he growled.

"Seeing as I can't get out of this house I'll compromise with you."

"Go on boy, I'm listening."

"Look I don't want to die, so if you promise not to kill me I'll come out."

"Yes, of course. I'm just jerking you around, I ain't gonna hurt you. Just come on out."

Jimmy creaked the bathroom door open slowly and eased out into the larger room.

"Like I said, I was just jerking you around, so come on over and get the keys out of my pocket," Tray Man flashed his rotted teeth in a loathsome grin.

Jimmy moved ever so slowly toward the table where the gruesome man sat like a mossy gargoyle. He was trying to buy time so Bobby could get into place.

"Well come on punk, before I change my mind!"

Jimmy reached out cautiously for his dirty vest pocket.

"Got ya dumb ass!" Tray Man's hand struck Jimmy's arm like a cobra and the bite was just as deadly. Jimmy shuddered and tried uselessly to break free of the firm grip.

"Some legs are coming off tonight, I promise you that boy." He had come within inches of Jimmy's face with this last threat, and his noxious breath made Jimmy want to vomit.

But before Jimmy became sick, he saw a slight movement by the door. It was Bobby sneaking up behind Tray Man with an empty bottle. His spirits immediately raised and a sudden confidence came over him.

"Up yours, you toothless, stinky, no leg, crippled creep!"

By this time Bobby was directly behind him with bottle raised in attack position when all of the sudden Tray Man turned around eye to eye with Bobby.

"Do it!" Jimmy shouted and shut his eyes tight. "Do it now!"

Only silence followed, so Jimmy squinted one eye to check out the situation.

"It's about time! This little punk was fixing to break free and bolt!"

Bobby was holding the stumpy half man in his arms. "Shut up! Have they ever gotten away before?" Bobby smirked.

"What's going on?" Jimmy blurted out.

"Let's get on with this." Bobby scowled and smashed Jimmy in the head with the bottle.

When Jimmy awakened he was tied to an old chair. Tray Man was on the autopsy table scrubbing it with alcohol and disinfectant. Bobby was passed out on a portable hospital gurney with a tall shadowy figure lurking over him with a stethoscope checking his breathing.

"We're ready to go," the man kissed Bobby on the cheek. "Everything is perfect, baby. Daddy's going to take care of everything."

"I'm all done here, Doc."

"There had better not be one germ on that table before I start, you hear me!"

"I told you I was done," Tray Man hissed.

The shadowy figure became motionless, statuesque in pose, then suddenly he backhanded Tray Man, sending him crashing into the chair that Jimmy was tied to.

"You broke my nose!" Tray Man whimpered in defeat.

The tall man converged on him like a bird of prey, heaving his fists and slamming him into the wall. "We wouldn't be here right now if it wasn't for your sorry drunk ass, now would we?"

Tray Man grimaced.

"If you hadn't stolen your father's car at age fourteen, gotten drunk and ran that red light, my little angel would still have *his* legs today! Even after I hacked your legs off for payback it just wasn't enough." He dropped the stumpy man to the ground with a thump and walked quietly back across to Bobby.

Jimmy was shocked beyond speech. He could do nothing but watch in horror as the man in black began to saw into Bobby's legs. Vomit rose from the pit of his stomach, and he went black again.

When Jimmy regained his senses, this time *he* was strapped down to the autopsy table. "What's going on?"

"Jimmy, my name is Dr. Robert Brock. I'm Bobby's Dad."

Jimmy's mind began to clear, and he remembered the predicament he was in.

"And since you're a bad little boy who smokes, drinks and disobeys his parents, like some other unbridled heathen I had the misfortune of meeting ten years ago," Dr. Brock cut his eyes over to Tray Man with malice, "I am going to saw your legs off and give them to a more deserving boy, like Bobby. After all, it is his birthday, and a growing boy needs a growing pair of legs doesn't he?"

"But the Tray Man? I saw the newspaper clipping on the wall!" Jimmy urged.

"Oh yes, the newspaper. It is correct," he grinned.

Jimmy retorted with a bewildered glance.

"The headline read: Drunk Driver Runs Into Prominent Doctor With Crippling Results. Did you bother to read the story?"

Jimmy returned the same dazed stare.

"What Bobby told you was just a lure, a line for hoodlum punks like you to hook on to. It did not happen quite the way it was described to you. Tray Man was the drunk driver, I was the prominent doctor, and my poor Bobby was the one who got his legs amputated!"

Jimmy shook violently as Dr. Brock stepped closer to him with bone saw in hand.

"You see I keep that monstrosity around to help me get the kids I need to transplant Bobby's legs every year on his birthday, and in turn I allow him to live. Pretty fair trade off, huh Tray Man?"

Tray Man whimpered and slumped back into the shadows.

"But, wait, I didn't mean to be, I mean I didn't do anything!" Jimmy tried to flounce off the table to no avail.

And without another instant of debate, Dr. Brock began to laugh psychotically as the fabric in Jimmy's shorts pressed deep into his thighs under the pressure of the saw.

-end-

About "Tray Man"
& Greg Burnham

The story has one dominant moral; bad things happen to naughty kids, so be sweet or the "boogey man" is going to get you. Jimmy's mother implied that he used to be a good boy, and now she just didn't understand his bad attitude. *He* is making the choice to change his disposition. This is reinforced when he makes his new friends and they immediately extend the opportunity to choose the wrong path, i.e. smoking, drinking, etc. Once again a choice made by Jimmy, so the underlying moral is that you are responsible for your own actions.

This was inspired by the sight of a man with the same physical description of "Tray Man" rooting around in a garbage bin down town. My mind immediately turned to thoughts of childhood fears, and how this guy would have scared the piss out of me when I was a kid. That in turn made me think of having to face this guy for being a bad little boy.

I have been married to my wife Mandy for nine years and we have two children, Megan age seven and Peyton age four. I am a Department Head at the University of South Alabama in Mobile and any and all of my hobbies are in direct relation to my children and what's relevant to them. You may know the feeling?

I have a short story entitled "I Know What Scares You" in the anthology *Cemetery Sonata*, edited by June Hubbard, published by Chameleon Publishing.

About the Artist - Marziah Karch

Marziah Karch is an artist currently living in Lawrence, Kansas with her husband, daughter, a pet iguana, and a guinea pig. She received her Bachelors in Fine Arts in Printmaking from the University of Kansas in 1995, and she's planning to complete a Masters in Instructional Design and Technology in May 2003.

Her awards for artwork include Best Science Fiction at Mage Con North IV, Best of Show at Mage Con North V, and Best Use of Color at Gateway 2.

Among her hobbies (which she has less and less time for, now that she's a mom), she enjoys going to various science fiction conventions, building computers from spare parts, reading voraciously, and collecting all the Buffy DVDs.

Yard Dog Press Titles
As Of This Print Date

(Continued on the next page)

Three Ways to Order:

1. Write us a letter telling us what you want, then send it along with your check or money order (made payable to Yard Dog Press) to: Yard Dog Press, 710 W. Redbud Lane, Alma, AR 72921-7247

2. Contact us at srosen.lstran@juno.com to place your order. Then send your check or money order to the address above. *This has the advantage of allowing you to check on the availability of short-stock items such as T-shirts and back-issues of Yard Dog Comics.*

3. Contact us as in #2 above and pay with a credit card or by debit from your checking account. Just go to our website and sign up for PayPal. It's free, it's safe, it's easy. If you already have a PayPal account, it's even easier!

Watch our website at
www.yarddogpress.com
for news of upcoming projects
and new titles!!

A Note to Our Readers

We at Yard Dog Press understand that many people buy used books because they simply can't afford new ones. That said, and understanding that not everyone is made of money, we'd like you to know something that you may not have realized. Writers only make money on new books that sell. At the big houses a writer's entire future can hinge on the number of books they sell. While this isn't the case at Yard Dog Press, the honest truth is that when you sell or trade your book or let many people read it, the writer and the publishing house aren't making any money.

As much as we'd all like to believe that we can exist on love and sweet potato pie, the truth is we all need money to buy the things essential to our daily lives. Writers and publishers are no different.

We realize that these "freebies" and cheap books often turn people on to new writers and books that they wouldn't other wise read. However we hope that you will reconsider selling your copy, and that if you trade it or let your friends borrow it, you also pass on the information that if they really like the author's work they should consider buying one of their books at full price sometime so that the writer can afford to continue to write work that entertains you.

We appreciate all our readers and *depend* upon their support.

Thanks,
The Editorial Staff
Yard Dog Press